a swell-looking babe

Other titles available in Vintage Crime/Black Lizard

a swell-looking babe

jim thompson

VINTAGE CRIME / **BLACK LIZARD**

vintage books · a division of random house, inc. · new york

First Vintage Crime/Black Lizard Edition, November 1991

Library of Congress Cataloging-in-Publication Data
Thompson, Jim, 1906–1977.
A swell-looking babe/by Jim Thompson. — 1st Vintage crime/Black Lizard ed.
p.   cm. —(Vintage crime/Black Lizard)
ISBN 0-679-73311-6
I. Title.   II. Series.
PS3539.H6733S9   1991
813'.54—dc20   91-50071 CIP

Manufactured in the United States of America
10 9 8 7 6 5 4 3 2 1

a swell-looking babe

He had dreamed about her. Now, waking to the sweaty southern night, he found both arms clasped around his pillow, the cloth wet with saliva where his mouth had pressed against it, and he flung it away from him with a mixture of disgust and disappointment. Some babe, he thought drowsily, his hand moving from bed lamp to alarm clock to cigarettes. A dream boat—and that's the way he'd better leave her. Right in the land of dreams. He had to keep the money coming in. He had to keep out of trouble. And he had been sternly advised, at the time of his employment by the Hotel Manton, that bellboys who attempted intimacies with lady guests invariably landed in serious trouble.

"This is what they call a tight hotel," the superintendent of service had explained. "A hooker never gets past the room clerk. Or if she does, she doesn't stay long and neither does he. It's just good business, get me, Rhodes? A guest may not be everything he should be himself, but he doesn't want to pay upwards of ten dollars a day for a room in a whore house."

"I understand," Dusty had said.

"We're not running any Sunday school, of course. As long as our guests are quiet about it, we'll put up with a little hanky-panky. But we don't—and you don't—mix into it, see? Don't get friendly with a woman, even if she does seem to invite it. You might be mistaken. She might change her mind. And the hotel would have a hell of a lawsuit on its hands."

Dusty had nodded again, his thin face slightly flushed with embarrassment. That had been almost a year ago, back before he had lost his capacity for being insulted, before he had learned simply to accept . . . and hate. He had thought the job only temporary then, something that paid well, without the business experience and references usually required in well-paying jobs. Mom had still been alive. Dad had stood a chance of being reinstated by the school board. He, Dusty, had had to drop out of school, but it would be only for a few months. So he had thought—or hoped. He was going to be a doctor, not merely a uniform with a number on it.

He had nodded his understanding, blushing, trying to cut short the interview. And the superintendent's face had softened, and he had called him by his first name.

"Are you sure you want to do this kind of work, Bill? I can fit you in as food checker or key clerk or something of that nature. Of course, it wouldn't pay nearly as much as you can make on tips, but . . . "

"Thank you," Dusty had said. "But I think I'd better take it, the job that pays the most money."

"Don't forget what I've said, then." The superintendent became impersonal again. "It's only fair to tell you, incidentally, that periodic checks are made on all our service employees."

"Checks?"

"Yes. By women detectives—spotters, we call 'em. So watch yourself when some prize looker makes a play for you. She may be working for the hotel."

Dusty had mumbled a promise to watch himself. Until last night, he had strictly adhered to that promise. It wasn't because of any want of temptation. As the superintendent had pointed out, the Manton wasn't running a Sunday school. It was exclusive largely via its room rates. You didn't have to show a financial statement or a marriage certificate to get a room. The Manton insisted not so much on respectability as the appearance of it; its concern was for its own welfare, not the morals of its guests.

Actually, Dusty supposed, the Manton got more than its share of the fast crowd; they preferred it to hotels with lower rates and virtually no restrictions. In any event, more than one woman guest had given him some pretty broad hints, and he'd let them slide right on past. Not because they might be spotters. He just hadn't been interested. In his sea of troubles, there'd been no room for women.

Then, last night . . .

Dusty yawned, glanced at the clock, and swung his feet out of bed. For a moment he remained perched on the edge of the mattress, absently wiggling his toes against the semi-cool bare floor. Then he stood up and padded into the bathroom.

He took a quick cold shower. He came out of the shower stall, and began to shave.

Even with his face lathered, tautened and twisted to receive the strokes of the razor, he was good-looking, and, more important, intelligent-looking. As a youngster, when the other kids had dubbed him with such hateful titles as Pretty Boy and Dolly, he had detested those good looks. And while he had eventually become resigned to them, he had always resented them. They could get him nothing he wanted, nothing, with ten years of college study to complete, that he had time for. After all, he was going to be a doctor, not an actor.

A year ago he had gone to work at the Manton, and gradually, through the months since then, it had been borne home to him that he was never going back to college, that he would never be a doctor. But that had not changed his attitude about his appearance. It set him apart from the other employees, at once arousing their resentment and precluding the anonymity which he sought. It brought unwanted and dangerous attentions from certain of the women guests.

It spelled nothing but trouble, and he was already knee-deep in trouble.

Then, last night had come, and for the first time in his life he was glad that he was as he was. After he had seen her, after what had happened last night . . .

He dashed water over his face, dried it, stood frowning at himself in the medicine-cabinet mirror. Silently, he advised his image to forget last night. A dame like that didn't go for bellboys. She might tease you along a little, but that would be the end of it. Or if it wasn't the end of it, if you could actually get a tumble from her, what of it? Nothing. Just a big fat headache. He might not be able to drop her, and he certainly couldn't hang onto her. For something he couldn't really have—just a taste of something that would leave him hungrier than ever—he'd risk losing his job. Maybe something a hell of a lot worse than that.

He returned to the bedroom, and started to dress: gray trousers, black-and-white sport shoes, blue shirt and black tie. He donned a blue flannel coat, tucked a white handkerchief into the breast pocket. He buttoned the second button absently, still worrying. Step by step, he thought back over last night's events.

According to her registry card, her name was Marcia Hillis and she was from Dallas, Texas. Dusty supposed that she must have hit town on the 11:55 train since she arrived at the hotel a little after midnight, a few minutes after he had gone to work. He swung the cab door open for her, lifting her luggage from the driver's compartment. Then, he stepped across the walk to the lobby entrance, at this door without its doorman, and pulled open the door there.

Smiling perfunctorily, he turned and waited for her.

She finished paying and tipping the driver. She came out of the dark interior of the cab and into the bright lights of the marquee. Dusty blinked. His heart popped up into his throat, then bounced down into the pit of his stomach. He almost dropped her luggage.

Sure, he'd seen some good-looking women before, at the Manton and away from it. He'd seen them, and they'd made it pretty obvious that they saw him. But he'd never come up against anything like this, a woman who was not just one but *all* women. That was the way he thought of her, right from the first moment. All women—the personification, the refined best of them all. She was twenty. She was thirty. She was sixty.

Her face, with the serene brown eyes and the deliciously curling lips: she was twenty in the face but without the vacuousness which often goes with twenty. Her body, compactly mature, was that of a woman of thirty but with none of thirty's sometime flabbiness. Her hair was sixty, he thought of it that way—or, rather, what sixty is portrayed as being in story and picture. Completely gray. Gray, but soft and lustrous. Not the usual dead, crackling harshness of gray.

She wore it in a long gleaming bob which almost brushed the shoulders of her tailored suit. He stared down at it as she passed him, and then still half-dazed he followed her into the lobby.

Apparently she had something of the same effect on Bascom, the room clerk, that she had on him, for he was shoving a registration card across the desk and extending a fountain pen while she was still a dozen feet away. That was so unusual as to be unheard of. Dusty couldn't remember when Bascom had rented a room to an unescorted woman. He got a kick out of turning them down. With Miss Marcia Hillis, however, he was all welcoming smiles. Moreover, he did not treat her to an icy stare, as he usually did in such cases, when she hesitated over the price of the room.

"Well, now, of course," he murmured, with unaccustomed unction. "Fifteen dollars is rather high. I believe . . . yes, I do have one room at ten. I'll let you have that."

Bascom assigned her to a room with southern exposure on the tenth, the top, floor. It was at the end of the corridor, a considerable walk from the elevator, and not too large, but it was undoubtedly the best of the Manton's ten-buck rooms. The city got hot as hell at this time of year, and high-up rooms on the south were at a premium.

Dusty preceded her down the long thickly carpeted hallway. He unlocked the door, flicked on the light and gestured without looking at her. She went in, brushing against him slightly as he stooped to pick up her baggage.

He placed the luggage—a suitcase, hat box and overnight case—on a stand immediately inside the door. He turned on the bathroom light, tested the circulating ice water spigot and checked the supply of towels and soap. He came out of the bath, edged toward the corridor door.

Breathing heavily. Still not looking at her.

A little red flag in his mind was swinging for all it was worth. He didn't want any tip from her, only to get out of there before something happened that had better not happen.

"I hope you'll be comfortable, ma'am," he said, and he got his hand on the doorknob. "Good night."

"Just a moment," she said, firmly. "Don't I have a fan in this room?"

"You won't need one," he said. "You get a very nice breeze on this side of the hotel."

"Oh? Well, will you open the windows, please?"

That was just what he didn't want to do, because she was standing by the bed, between the bed and the chest of drawers, and that left very little room for him to pass her. And he knew, as well as he knew he couldn't trust himself far with this babe, that she wasn't going to move out of the way.

He hesitated for a moment, his eyes concentrating on a spot directly above that lustrous gray head, but of course he couldn't refuse. He squeezed past her hurriedly, so brusquely that her knees bent and she almost toppled backward to the bed. He flung the windows up, and the strong south breeze swept in . . . slamming the door.

He turned around, looking directly at her at last.

She was facing him now. There was a fifty-cent piece between the tapering fingers of her extended right hand.

"Thank you, very much," she said. "Who shall I call for — in case I want anything else?"

"I".—he licked his lips— "I'm the only bellboy on at night. You won't need to call by name."

She looked at him silently. She stared straight into his eyes, holding them, and came toward him. The extended hand lowered, went into the pocket of his trousers, placing the tip there. It remained there, deep in his pocket.

"Dusty"—he blurted the word out. He had to do something, say something, before he exploded. "I m-mean it's Bill, but my last name's Rhodes so everyone calls me D-Dus—"

"I see." Her eyes narrowed drowsily, her hand still in his pocket. "What time do you get off work, Dusty?"

"S-seven. I work from midnight to seven."

"'I'll bet you get awfully lonesome, don't you, roaming through a big hotel at night all by yourself? Don't you get lonesome, Dusty?"

"L-look," he stammered. "Look, Miss. I—"

"But you wouldn't be lonesome long," she said. "Not a guy who looks like you."

She leaned into him. Suddenly, because by God he couldn't help it, his arms went around her, right around those smoothly curving hips. And just as suddenly . . .

Just as suddenly she was standing six feet away from him. Over by the windows. And her voice and face were as cool as the insweeping breeze.

"Did I give you your tip?" she said. "I believe that will be all, then."

That brought him up short. It was as though he'd been jerked out of an oven and into an ice box. He turned toward the door, angry, disappointed, and also relieved. Nothing could come of a deal like this. She was trouble. He couldn't afford trouble.

He shivered a little, thinking of what might have happened if she hadn't turned frosty on him. Relieved that it hadn't happened. Empty-feeling and disappointed because it hadn't.

He reached the door. She spoke again, and again her voice was warm, drowsy, filled with promise.

"That will be all," she repeated. "Now."

Slowly, he turned around.

She was still standing by the windows, and the wind was swirling the long white curtains around her, draping the rich body, ruffling the lustrous white hair. There against the background of the night, molded by the wind-blown curtains, she was like one of those unbelievably beautiful manatees from the prow of some Viking vessel. Or, no that wasn't right; she was too alive for that. She was like one of those ancient goddesses who tired of their heavenly pleasures and came down to earth for the delights of Man. Venus. Ceres, the Earth Mother. All things that were woman, eternal but never aging.

"Now," she said. "Nothing else now, Dusty."

And she laughed in a gently mocking way.

He let the door slam behind him. Rather, he slammed it.

He cursed her all the way to the elevator.

It didn't seem possible, but almost fifteen minutes had passed since he'd left the lobby. Behind the long marble desk, Bascom beckoned to him grimly.

"Where have you been?" he snapped. "What were you doing up in that room all this time?"

"Had to get some towels from the linen room," Dusty lied. "I guess the maid must have slipped up."

"You're sure *you* didn't slip up?"

"Just the maid," Dusty grinned at him, "and possibly you."

Bascom's mouth tightened. His eyes shifted uncomfortably.

Like many first-class hotels, the Manton had very few

rooms at its lowest advertised rate. In fact, in the case of the Manton, there were only six rooms which rented for the ten-dollar minimum. They were by way of being prizes, something to be doled out to long-time patrons of the hotel. Never, to the best of Dusty's recollection, had one been rented at night. They didn't have to be. A guest hitting town late at night could and would pay practically anything he was asked to.

Bascom had slipped, then. He'd made a double slip. He'd not only deprived the hotel of the extra revenue deriving from a more expensive room, but he'd also—potentially but inevitably—disappointed a preferred guest. The guest wouldn't like that— The day clerks wouldn't like it. The management wouldn't like it. In view of the Manton's room turnover, of course, Bascom's lapse stood every chance of going unmarked. But if Dusty should happen to mention it, very casually, needless to say . . .

Bascom turned on his heel and went up into the cashier's cage. After a moment, he called to Dusty to come help him with the transcript sheets. That was the way the matter ended.

Anyway, Dusty guessed—as he studied himself in the dresser mirror—he wasn't in any trouble. If she'd been a teaser, one of those dames who worked you into making a pass and then squawked to the management, she'd have done her kicking last night. It didn't take a woman seven hours to decide she'd been insulted.

He heard the screen door to the front porch open, and his father's dragging footsteps. He frowned, irritably, still thinking about her and hating this interruption.

Who was she anyway, this Miss Marcia Hillis, of Dallas, Texas? What was she? Not a hooker, certainly. She hadn't propositioned him, and you learned to spot a hustling woman fast around a hotel. It didn't make any difference how they dressed, how high-toned they acted. You could spot them a mile away.

She wasn't a spotter—a detective—for the hotel, either. If she had been, she wouldn't have quibbled over the room rate. There would have been no reason to since the house would pick up her bill.

A business woman, then? Nope, she didn't use the right

lingo, and business people didn't arrive at a hotel late at night without reservations.

A tourist? No, again; there was nothing in this town to attract a tourist, and, at any rate, he just couldn't picture her as a sightseer.

One of the horse-racing crowd? Well, yes, she could fit in with them, the upper-class stratum of them which made Hotel Manton its headquarters. She could, but he knew she didn't. The racing season didn't start for at least two weeks.

Probably, Dusty decided, she was just a woman at loose ends. Hungering for adventure, but afraid of it. Wandering aimlessly from one place to another, with nothing to do and all the time in the world to do it in.

So . . . so what difference did it make? Whoever or whatever she was, he'd never let her get him into another spot like the one last night. If she tried anything like that again, and for all he knew she might have checked out during the day—he'd put a freeze on her that would give her pneumonia.

. . . There was a tired apologetic cough from the bedroom doorway.

Frowning, Dusty turned and faced his father.

Of course, the old man was sick, much, much sicker than he realized. But that still could not account for his appearance; it did not, in Dusty's opinion, excuse that appearance. He had begun to let himself go after his dismissal from the city schools; then, his wife—Dusty's foster mother—had died and he had let go completely.

He went days on end without shaving, weeks without a haircut. His soiled baggy clothes looked like they'd been slept in. He looked like a tramp—like a scarecrow out of a cornfield. And that wasn't the worst of it. The worst was what he'd let happen to himself mentally. He seemed to take pride in being absent-minded, in seeing how stupidly he could do the few things that were left for him to do.

Why, good God, Dusty thought. His father was only a little past sixty, and he was practically senile. He couldn't be
trusted with the simplest task. You couldn't send him to the
store after a cake of soap and have him come back with the
right change.

"Well"—Dusty forced the frown from his face. "How's it
going, Dad?"

"Pretty good, Bill. Did you sleep well?"

"Not bad. As good as I could in this weather."

Mr. Rhodes nodded absently. A streak of saliva curved
down from the corner of his mouth, and he wiped at his
chin with the back of his hand.

"I got another letter from the lawyers today, Bill. They
think that—"

"Have we got anything to eat in the house?" Dusty interrupted. "Anything I can make a sandwich out of?"

"I wanted to tell you, Bill. They think—"

Dusty interrupted him again. He knew what the lawyers
thought, the same thing they always thought: that his
father's case should be appealed to a higher court; that he,
Dusty, was a sucker who could be conned indefinitely into
paying their legal fees.

"Dad!" he said sharply. "We'll talk about the lawyers
another time. Right now I want to know why we don't have
any food. What did you do with the money I gave you?"

"Why, I—I—" The old man's eyes were blank, childishly
bewildered. "Now, what did I—"

"Never mind," Dusty sighed. "Skip it. But you did get
something to eat yourself, didn't you? You did, didn't you
Dad?"

"Why—oh, yes," Mr. Rhodes said quickly. Too quickly.
"I've eaten very well today."

"What, for example? You bought just enough groceries
for yourself—is that what you're telling me, Dad?"

"Ye—I mean, no." Mr. Rhodes' eyes avoided his son's. "I
ate out. It was too hot to do any cooking, so I—"

"You ate at Pete's place?"

"Yes—no. No, I didn't eat at Pete's." His father shied
away from the trap. Dusty might check at the neighborhood lunchroom. "I went to another place, down toward
town."

Dusty studied him wearily. He refrained from asking the name of the restaurant. It was no use—at such times as this his father was like a sly child—and he just wasn't capable of it. No matter how provoked you got, you shouldn't badger your own dad.

"All right," he said quietly, taking his billfold from his pocket. "Here's a couple dollars. Go down to Pete's and get you a good meal. Right now, Dad, before you go to bed. Will you do that?"

"Certainly. Of course I will, Bill." Mr. Rhodes almost snatched the money from his hand. "Will it be all right if—if—?"

Dusty hesitated over the unspoken question. "Well," he said, slowly. "You know what we decided about that, Dad. We both agreed on it, that it just wasn't a good idea. When a man's out of work, when he's worried, it's pretty easy to . . ."

"But I was just going to get a beer, just sit at the bar a while and watch television."

"I know, but—"

"But what?" There was an unaccustomed sharpness in his father's voice. "I don't understand you, Bill. Why all this fuss over a bottle of beer? You know I've never been a heavy drinker. I just don't have any taste for the stuff. But the way you've harped on the subject lately, you'd think I—"

"I'm sorry." Dusty clapped him on the back, urged him toward the door. "I just get tired and worried, and I talk too much. Go on and have your beer, Dad. But get you a good meal, too."

"But I'd like to know why—"

"No reason. Like I said, I talk too much. You run along, and I'll see you in the morning."

Mr. Rhodes left, still muttering annoyedly. Dusty remained in the house a few minutes longer, giving him time to get out of sight. The old man had gotten dangerously suspicious a moment ago. It wouldn't do to feed those suspicions further by having him think he was being followed.

Dusty fixed and drank a glass of ice water while he waited. Ice, by God, was just about all there was in the refrigerator. He smoked a cigarette, pacing back and forth across the shabby living room. At last, after a nervous glance at his wrist watch, he hurried out of the house and jumped into his car.

At a drive-in restaurant, he gulped down a hot turkey sandwich and two cups of coffee. He parked his car at the rear of the Manton, hurried through the service entrance and on into the locker room. There was a sour taste in his mouth. The food he had eaten lay heavy on his stomach. He was tired, sweaty. He felt like he had never rested, never bathed.

Stripping out of his clothes, he took another shower—cold and necessarily quick. He dried himself, standing directly beneath the ceiling fan. He put on his wine-colored, tuxedo-like uniform, and hung his street clothes in his locker. He sat down under the fan, tapping the persistent sweat from his face with his bath towel. It was ten, no nine, minutes of twelve. There was time for another smoke, time to pull himself together a little before he went up to the lobby.

He lighted a cigarette moodily, broodingly, trying to escape from the feeling of sullen despair, of hopeless frustration, which crept over him more and more of late.

There was no way out that he could see. No exit from his difficulties. His mind traveled in a circle, beginning and ending with his father. The doctor bills, the medicines, the frittering away of money almost as fast as it could be made. Two dollars, five dollars, ten dollars, whatever you gave the old man, he got rid of. And he wasn't a damned bit hesitant about asking for more.

Dusty had considered taking a day job. But day bellboys didn't make as much money, and they had to work split watches. He'd have to be away from home practically as much as he was now. . . . Hire a housekeeper? Well, how would that help? Thirty-five or forty bucks a week in salary, and you'd have to feed her besides. Anyway, dammit, it just wasn't necessary. None of this nonsense, which kept him drained of money, was necessary. His father was sharp enough when he chose to be. He'd proved that tonight. The trouble was that he, Dusty, had just babied and humored the old man so much that . . .

"Hey, Rhodes! How about it?" It was the day captain,

shouting down from the top of the service steps.

Dusty shouted, "Coming!" and left the locker room. But he ascended the long stairway unhurriedly, wrapped in thought.

His father couldn't be losing and mislaying and generally mismanaging to the extent that he appeared to be. He must be spending the money on something. But what in the world would a man his age—

Suddenly, Dusty knew. The answer to the riddle was so damned obvious. Why the hell hadn't he thought of it before this?

The day bellboys swept past him on the steps. Lighting cigarettes, peeling out of their jackets and collars as they hastened toward the locker room. A few spoke or nodded to him. They got no greeting in return. He was too choked up, blind with anger.

Those lawyers, those dirty thieving shysters! That was where the money was going.

Well, he'd put a stop to that. There would be no use in jumping his father about it; he couldn't really blame his father for doing what he undoubtedly had. It was their fault—the lawyers—for holding out hope to him. And they'd darned well better lay off if they knew what was good for them. He'd write 'em a letter that would curl their hair. Or, no, he'd pay them a little visit. He wanted to tell those birds off personally.

Opening the door of the service landing, he entered the lobby, his anger dying and with it the sense of frustration. He paused at the end of the long marble desk untended now except by sour old Bascom—and looked down at the open pages of the room-call ledger.

She was still here, he saw. A bellboy had taken cigarettes and a magazine to her room fifteen minutes ago. Up at 11:45, down at 11:50; just long enough to complete the errand. Not long enough for anything . . . anything else. And, yes, that was the only boy to go to her room today.

Dusty didn't know why he felt good about it, because of course—she couldn't mean anything to him; he was shying clear of that baby. But somehow he did feel good. Here was proof positive that she wasn't a hooker or spotter, proof that he was the only guy in the place that she had any interest in.

A cab honked at the side door. Grinning unconsciously, Dusty hurried across the lobby and down the steps.

As modern hotels go, the Manton was not a large place. Its letterheads boasted of "four hundred rooms, four hundred baths." Actually, there were three hundred and sixty-two, and since any number of these were linked together into suites, the baths totaled far less than three hundred and sixty-two.

The Manton—or rather the company which operated it— had learned the advantage in renting two rooms to one person rather than two rooms to two persons. It had learned the vast difference in profit between renting two rooms at five dollars and one at ten dollars. It had learned that the man who pays five dollars for a room is apt to be much more demanding than the one who pays ten.

The Manton was seldom rented to capacity. It did not have to be. With only two-thirds of its rooms rented, its income was equal to that of a larger, fully-occupied—and less "exclusive"—hotel. Also, since the number of a hotel's employees is inevitably geared to the number of its guests, its overhead was much lower.

Bascom was the sole front-office employee after midnight, performing—with Dusty's assistance—the duties of room clerk, key clerk, cashier and night auditor. There was no night house detective. The coffee shop and grille room closed at one o'clock. By two, the lobby porters had completed their mopping and scrubbing and were on their way homeward. At two, the late-shift elevator operator left, and Dusty took care of his infrequent calls from then on.

It was a little before two when Tug Trowbridge came in. While his two companions—you seldom saw him alone — sauntered on a few steps, Tug stopped at the cashier's cage where Dusty and Bascom were working. He was a big, almost perpetually smiling man, with a shock of red hair and a hearty, booming voice. Now, as Dusty grinned obediently and Bascom smirked nervously, he triggered an enormous forefinger at the clerk.

"Okay, Dusty boy"—he scowled with false menace—"I got him covered. Grab the keys and clean out those safety-deposit boxes."

Dusty stretched his grin into an appreciative laugh. Tug's joke was an old one, but he was the best tipper in the Manton. "Can't do it, Mr. Trowbridge, remember? It takes two different keys for each box."

"Now, by God!" Tug slapped his forehead in a gesture of dismay. "Why can't I ever remember that!"

He guffawed, putting a period to the joke. Then, he dug a small, flat key from his vest and shoved it through the wicket. "A little service, hey, brother Bascom? Got something that's kind of weighing me down."

"Yes, sir," said Bascom obsequiously.

There was a ledger, indexing the depositors in the chilled-steel boxes which formed the rear wall of the cashier's cage. But it was unnecessary to consult this, of course, in the case of a regular like Tug Trowbridge. Bascom took a heavy ring of keys from his cash drawer, and selected one with a certain number—a number, incidentally, which did *not* correspond to the one on Tug's key. Turning to the rear of the enclosure, he found Tug's box number—and this also was different from that of either of the two keys—and unlocked its two locks. He pulled the box out of its niche, and set it in the window in front of Trowbridge.

Dusty averted his eyes, tactfully, but not before he had got a glimpse of the sheaf of bills which Tug casually tossed into the box. It was almost an inch thick, wrapped around at the ends with transparent tape. There was a thousand-dollar bill on top.

Bascom put the box back into place, and carefully relocked it. He returned Tug's key, dropping the others back into the cash drawer.

"Well, Dusty"—Trowbridge gave the bellboy a wink "I guess you're right. No use knocking over Bascom here unless we could get ahold of the other keys."

"No, sir," Dusty smiled.

"And how we going to do that, hey? How we going to know who's got keys and whether they got anything worth getting?"

"That's right," said Dusty.

Bascom was trying to smile, but the effort was not very successful. Tug winked at Dusty.

"Looks like we're making our pal a little nervous," he said. "Maybe we better lay off before he calls the cops on us."

"Oh, no," Bascom protested. He had about as much sense of humor, in Dusty's opinion, as one of the lobby sand-jars. "It's just that when a man's alone here at night—practically alone all night long—and he's responsible for all this—"

"Sure," Trowbridge nodded good-humoredly. "Jokes about hold-ups aren't very funny."

"As a matter of fact," Bascom continued seriously, "I don't believe there's ever been a successful hold-up of a major hotel. You see—"

"No kidding," said Trowbridge, his voice faintly sarcastic. "Well, thanks for letting me know."

"Oh, I didn't mean that—"

"Sure, sure. I know." Trowbridge laughed again, but not too jovially. "Come up to the suite after a while, huh, Dusty? Make it about a half hour. Got some laundry I want you to pick up."

"Yes, sir," said Dusty.

Trowbridge rejoined his two companions. Bascom watched them as they proceeded on down the lobby to the bank of elevators beneath the mezzanine. There was a drawn look about his prim humorless face. He was breathing a little heavily, his thin pinched nostrils flaring with annoyance.

Dusty studied him covertly, grinning to himself. Bascom had better watch his step. Tug Trowbridge definitely wasn't a guy you'd want to get down on you.

Back in prohibition days, Tug had headed a statewide bootleg syndicate. His well-earned reputation for toughness was such as to make even the Capones shy away from him. During the war—though he had never been convicted—he had been the brains, and no small part of the muscle, of a group of black-market mobsters, men who specialized in the daylight hijacking of bonded whiskey trucks. At various times in his career, he had been involved—reputedly—in the loan-shark and slot-machine rackets.

These illegal and often deadly activities, or, more properly, these *alleged* activities, were now years behind him. His present and obviously profitable enterprises were confined to a juke-box company and a stevedoring firm. Still, and despite his brimming good humor, he obviously was not a man to be trifled with. Dusty knew that from the attitude of the men who accompanied him.

It wasn't likely, of course, that Tug would ever rough up Bascom. He'd be too contemptuous of the clerk, and there was an easier way of showing his displeasure.

Tug paid seven hundred and fifty dollars a month rent. His bar and restaurant bills ran at least as much more. Neither he nor his associates ever created a disturbance. He made no special demands on the hotel. In short, he was the Manton's idea of a highly desirable—a "respectable"—guest; and it would take no more than a word from him to get Bascom discharged.

. . . Dusty didn't get up to the Trowbridge suite within the half hour suggested. First, he had a hurry-up call for some aspirin from another room. Next, he had to unlock the check room for an early-departing guest, locate a small trunk stored therein and lug it out to the man's car. Then, there was a flurry of elevator traffic, now his responsibility since the operator had gone home.

It was Bascom, however, who was the chief cause of the delay. The clerk had insisted that Dusty give him the few minutes help he needed to complete the transcript. Then, with the task completed, he had pretended that the lock to the cashier's cage was jammed. Anyway, Dusty was convinced that it was a pretense. Bascom wouldn't let him try to work the key. He couldn't climb out of the enclosure, as he might have in any of the other front offices, because of the heavy steel netting across the top.

Finally, after almost twenty minutes had passed, the room clerk's phone rang, and, lo and behold, the lock suddenly became unjammed. Bascom gave him a shrewish, over-the-shoulder grin as he sauntered out of the cage. Dusty shoved past him roughly as the clerk began relocking the door.

It was in his mind to tell Trowbridge what had happened. But he wasn't quite angry enough for that, and, as it turned out, there was neither opportunity nor necessity to do so.

Tug and the other two men were lounging in the parlor of his suite, their coats off, brimming glasses in their hands. They were obviously unaware that Dusty was more than thirty minutes late.

"Here already, huh?" Tug beamed. "Now, that's what I call service. Sit down and have a drink with us."

"Thanks very much," said Dusty. "I don't drink, Mr. Trowbridge."

"Sure, you don't; keep forgetting," the big man nodded. "Well, have a smoke then. Shake hands with my friends. Don't believe you've met these gents."

Dusty shook hands with them, and sat down. He'd never seen them before, but he felt that he had. There was something in the manner of Tug's friends that made them all look a little alike.

"Dusty's the lad I started to tell you about," Trowbridge continued. "Ain't that hell, though? Here's a plenty smart kid, got almost four years of college under his belt, and he winds up hopping bells. Nice, huh? Some future for a guy that figured on being a doctor."

The two men looked sympathetic. Or, rather, they tried to. Tug wagged his head regretfully.

"That's about the way it stacks up, eh, Dusty? Your old man doesn't stand a chance of getting things straightened out?"

"It wouldn't do much good if he could," Dusty shrugged. "He'll never be well enough to go back to work."

"A hell of a note," mused Trowbridge. "I remember readin' about it at the time. I said to myself right then, Now, why the hell does a man want to do a thing like that? A man with a good job and a family to take care of. What's he figure it's going to get him to mix himself up with a bunch of Reds?"

"He didn't mix with any Reds," Dusty said quickly, almost sharply. "I know they tried to make it look that way, but it wasn't anything like that. You see there was this group—the Free Speech Committee—who wanted to hold a meeting in the school auditorium, and all Dad did was sign a petition to—"

"Sure"—Tug stifled a yawn. "Well, it was a lousy break,

anyway. Lousy for you. Of course, it was hard on your old man, too, but he'd already lived most of his life. The way I see it, he stuck his neck out and yours got stepped on."

"Well . . . " Dusty murmured. There was a casual bluntness about Trowbridge which precluded argument. For that matter, he didn't entirely disagree with the ex-racketeer.

Trowbridge got the bag of laundry from the bedroom, and gave him a dollar tip. He returned to the lobby, heartened by his talk with Tug yet vaguely ashamed of himself. His father hadn't done anything wrong. In any event, it wasn't up to Tug Trowbridge to pass judgment on him. Still, it was nice to have someone see your side of things, to realize that you were making a hell of a sacrifice and getting nothing for it. Everyone else—the doctor and the lawyers and his father, and his mother, up until the time of her death—had taken what he had done for granted.

Dusty couldn't remember just how he'd happened to tell Tug about the matter. It had just slipped out somehow, he guessed, a natural consequence of the big man's friendliness and interest. Trowbridge was a far cry from the Manton's average guest. He treated you like a friend, introduced you to the people he had with him. When he said, "How's it going?" or "What's on your mind, Dusty?" he really wanted to know. Or he certainly made it sound like he did.

 . . . Bascom was waiting for him when he got downstairs, frowning and tapping impatiently on the counter. "Finally got back, did you?" he said grimly. "How long does it take you to pick up a bag of laundry?"

"Not too long." Dusty looked at him coolly. "About as long as it takes you to unlock a door."

Bascom's eyes flashed. He flipped a slip of paper across the counter. "College boys," he jeered. "There's some calls for you, college boy. See if you can take care of them between now and daylight."

"Look, Mr. Bascom"—Dusty picked up the call slip. "What's . . . well, what's wrong, anyway? What are you sore at me about? We used to get along so well together, but every time I turn around now you—"

"Yes?" said Bascom. "If you don't like it, why don't you quit?"

"But I don't understand. If I've done or said anything—"

"Get moving," said Bascom crisply. "Step on it, or you won't get a chance to quit."

Dusty made the two calls—ice to one room, a telegram pick-up from another. This was another thing he couldn't remember: just how his quarreling with Bascom had started. It had begun only recently, he knew that. They'd gotten along swell for months, and then, apparently for no reason at all, Bascom had changed. And since then he could do nothing but scold and snarl and ridicule. Make things tougher than they were already.

Dusty had been pretty hurt at first. He still was. But the hurt was giving way to anger, a stubborn determination to stand up against the clerk's injustice. He didn't know what it was all about—and he was ceasing to care—but he knew that Bascom couldn't get him fired. Not, anyway, without digging up much more serious charges than he could make now. Dusty had broken various of the hotel's innumerable rules, as in the instances, for example, of smoking behind the key rack and working without his collar. But Bascom was guilty of some rule-breaking himself. Bascom wasn't supposed to slip up to an empty room for a quick shower. He wasn't supposed to trot down the street to an all-night lunch room instead of having his food sent in. Dusty always knew where he was, of course, and could get him back to the desk with a phone call within the space of two or three minutes. But that could make no difference to the hotel. Bascom was supposed to remain behind the counter throughout his shift. That was the rule, period. If the management ever found out—

Dusty completed the two calls, and returned to the desk. He and Bascom resumed the night's chores, interrupted now and then when Dusty had to leave on a room call or one of the telephones rang. They checked off the day's charge slips against the guests' bills. They checked the room rack against the information racks. The work went rapidly, Dusty calling out the data, Bascom checking it. In the pre-dawn stillness, the bellboy's clear steady monotone echoed through the desk area:

"Haines, eight fourteen, one at twelve dollars . . . Haley, nine twelve, Mr. and Mrs., two at fifteen . . . Heller, six fifty and fifty-two, one at eighteen . . . Hillis, Dallas, Tex.—"

"Wait a minute!" Bascom flung down his pencil. "What kind of a room number is Dallas, Tex.? If you can't do any better than that, I'll—"

"Sorry," Dusty said quickly. "Hillis, ten oh four, one at ten."

Bascom picked up the pencil. Then, suddenly, he laughed. Softly, amusedly. Suddenly—for the moment, at least—he was the old Bascom again.

"Out of this world, wasn't she?" he said. "I don't think I've ever seen a woman who could come up to her."

"I *know* I haven't," said Dusty.

"Yes, sir, a lovely woman," mused Bascom. "Everything a woman should be. You know, Bill"—he turned on his stool and faced Dusty—"have you any idea how it feels to be my age, in the job I'm in, and to see someone like her? I've used up my chances. I'm not an old man, but I'll never amount to anything more than I do now. And that isn't enough by a million miles for a woman like that. . . . It's not a nice feeling, Bill. Take my word for it."

Dusty nodded, slowly, still taken aback by the clerk's sudden change in manner. He could see what Bascom was driving at, but—

"You've been here about a year," Bascom went on. "How long do you intend to stay?"

"Well"—Dusty hesitated—"I don't know. I can't say, exactly. It depends on my father, how my expenses run and—"

"Does it? I've seen you on the street, Bill, the way you dress, your car. I've got a pretty good idea of what you make here—around a hundred and fifty a week, isn't it? That's what's actually keeping you here, the money. Plenty of money with no real work or responsibilities attached to it. A nice soft job with a lot of so-called big shots calling you by your first name. You don't want to give it up. If you did, you'd have gone back to school long ago."

"Oh, yeah?" Dusty reddened. And then he checked himself. "I mean, I know you're just trying to help me, Mr. Bascom, and I appreciate it. But—"

"I know. You've got doctor bills, your father to take care

of. But you could still swing it, Bill. There's such a thing as a student loan. Scholarships. You used to talk quite a bit about them when you first came here. There are part-time jobs you could get. You'd have to do plenty of scrimping and sacrificing, but if you really wanted to—"

"I couldn't. I can't!" Dusty protested. "'Why the doctor bills alone, those and the medicines, take—"

"Doctors will wait for their money, if it's in a good cause. There's a city dispensary for people with low incomes. So"—Bascom's eyebrows rose—"what else is there? A place to sleep, something to eat. That's about the size of it, isn't it? Don't tell me you couldn't manage that in these times. You could squeeze by for a few years, long enough to get your education."

Dusty wet his lips, hesitantly. Bascom made things sound awfully easy. If he had to do them himself, well . . .

"It's not that simple," he said. "There are plenty of things besides—"

"There always are. But there aren't many that you can't do without. No, Bill. It wouldn't be easy, not an ideal arrangement by any means. But . . . " His voice died. The friendliness went out of his face. "Forget it," he said coldly. "Let's get back to work."

"But I was going to say that—"

"I said to forget it," Bascom snapped. "You're lazy. You feel sorry for yourself. You want something for nothing. It's a waste of time talking to you. Now, call those rooms off to me, and call 'em off right."

Dusty gulped and swallowed. Voice shaking, he resumed the calling.

The remaining three hours of the shift passed swiftly. At five-thirty, the split-watch elevator boy arrived. At six, the head baggage porter retrieved the check-room key from Dusty and began his day's duties. At seven the entire day shift came to work.

In the locker room, Dusty took another shower and changed into his street clothes. He scowled at himself in the mirror, ripped out an abrupt disgusted curse.

He's right, old Bascom's right, he thought. No wonder he doesn't have any use for me. Dad and I could manage. We—he— couldn't spend what I didn't have. He'd probably pull himself together if I went back to school, if he knew that one of us was going to amount to something. It would give him something to live for.

He finished dressing, and went out to his car. Pulling away from the curb, he gave the Hotel Manton a knowing, deprecating look. It could go to hell, the Manton could, and Marcia Hillis along with it.

It was a shabby, rundown house, a faded-blue cottage, in a block that was barely a half-block. It was bordered on one side by a vacant lot, a hundred squarefoot jungle of weeds and Johnson grass, on the other by a crumbling brick warehouse. Facing it, across the narrow street, was a used-car lot. Dusty had rented the place shortly after his mother's death. Its chief—rather, its only—advantages were its cheapness and its distance, *per se* and socially, from the family's former neighborhood. Things had gotten pretty uncomfortable there after his father's trouble. In this section of town, there was little chance of encountering one-time friends.

Dusty ate breakfast on the way home, and it was nearly nine when he arrived. It was Wednesday, one of the two days a week that the doctor called, and a black coupe, with the letters MD on the license plate, was parked in front of the house. Dusty drew up behind it, waited until the doctor came out.

Doctor Lane was a brisk, chubby man with narrowed irritable-looking eyes. He bustled out to his car, frowning impatiently when Dusty intercepted him.

"Well, he's all right," he said brusquely. "As good as can be expected. Incidentally, can't you spruce him up a little? Can't expect a man to feel good when he goes around like a tramp."

"I'm doing the best I can." Dusty flushed. "I give him plenty of—"

"The best you can, eh?" The doctor looked him up and down. "Better try a little harder. Or else get someone in to look after him. Should be able to afford it."

He nodded curtly, and tossed his black-leather bag onto the seat of the car. His hand on the door, he paused and turned.

"Understand he's been having a little beer. Well, won't hurt him any. Won't do him any good, but there's damned little that will. Not enough alcohol in the slop they make these days to hurt a baby."

"I wanted to ask you, Doctor. If it's as dangerous as you say—"

"As I *say*?" Doctor Lane snapped. "Any considerable amount of alcohol will kill him. Stop his heart like that."

"Well, don't you think it would be better—safer—if he was told—"

"No, I don't think so. If I did I'd have told him before now." The doctor sighed wearily, obviously struggling to control his impatience. "Don't want to alarm him. You can understand that, can't you? Not the slightest need to tell him. He's a naturally careful liver. Doesn't smoke. Goes easy on the coffee. Gets plenty of rest . . . By the way, he's just as well off if he doesn't eat much. Doesn't do enough to burn it up. Okay? That doesn't make you mad, does it?"

"I—" Dusty's mouth snapped shut. He stared at Lane steadily. "Just what," he said, "do you mean by that?"

"Well—uh—" The doctor cleared his throat. "No offense. I only meant that working nights, and all, it was probably difficult for you to—to—"

"I see. I thought that's what you must mean, Doctor."

Doctor Lane laughed uneasily. "Now—uh—I was saying about the liquor. Only danger in it I see is, uh, negative, largely negative. Know what I mean? Explaining why he shouldn't have it. Alarming him. Mustn't do that, understand? No reason to do it. He's never drunk the stuff, no reason why he should take on any fatal quantity now. If he had any money to throw away, he'd—" The doctor broke off abruptly. He cleared his throat again. "As I was saying. My thought in warning you was that you might, with the best of intentions, urge some on him. I mean to say that, for example, you might be having some people in, and if you were drinking yourselves you'd naturally offer your father—"

"I don't drink, Doctor. I don't do any entertaining."

"Fine. Splendid. No cause for worry, then." Doctor Lane backed away a step. "Anything else?"

Dusty shook his head. There had been something, but he couldn't mention it now. Perhaps he could do it later, but he was in no mood now to ask for favors from Doctor Lane now. Probably it wouldn't do any good if he did ask. If Lane thought he was so lowdown as to mistreat his own father, he'd hardly be inclined to wait indefinitely on payment for his services.

Going up the walk to the house, Dusty guessed that he'd mismanaged the whole interview. The doctor was always cranky, ready to leap down your throat, at this hour of the morning. If he'd had to talk to him—and he might have waited until another time—he shouldn't have disputed with him, made the doctor humble himself for a curtness that was more or less normal for him.

Mr. Rhodes was seated on the living room lounge, squinting at the morning newspaper. He smiled absently at his son, and Dusty went on back to the kitchen. The coffee pot was still warm, and there was a little coffee still left in it. Dusty poured a cup, and carried it into the living room.

"Dad," he said. Then, sharply, "Dad! I want to talk to you."

"Oh!" The old man laid the paper aside reluctantly. "Go right ahead, Bill."

"I want you to gather up all your clothes today, all your laundry. I—maybe you'd better do it right away. I'll have the stuff picked up this morning, so we can get it back tomorrow."

"All right, son," his father said, mildly. "Do you want any of your things to go, too?"

"Just yours. The hotel still does mine at half price."

Mr. Rhodes shuffled out of the room. Dusty took up a sip of coffee, and picked up the telephone. He called the laundry and cleaners. Then he consulted the telephone directory, and, swallowing the rest of his coffee, called a grocery store.

He was just hanging up when his father returned. He lighted a cigarette, motioned for the old man to sit down.

"I've just ordered some groceries, Dad. They'll be delivered within the hour—twenty-three dollars and eight cents worth—and the man will have to have his money upon delivery. Now I can leave the money with you for him, and go on to bed, if you're sure you can take care of it. Otherwise, I'll sit up and wait."

"Of course, I can take care of it," said Mr. Rhodes. "You go get your sleep, Bill."

"Another thing. While you're waiting, I'd like to have you shave. I'll put a new blade in the razor for you. Draw the water if you want me to. Will you do that, Dad?"

"Well, I—" Mr. Rhodes ran a hand over his stubbled face. "That's—it's pretty hard for me to do, son. I—I have a hard time seeing what I'm doing since I broke my glasses."

"But you . . . You didn't have them fixed, Dad? After I gave you the money, and you promised—" Dusty broke off, abruptly. "All right," he said. "All right. You go in and see the optometrist tomorrow, have him give me a ring here at the house and tell me what the bill will be. I'll get a money order for you to give him when you pick up the glasses."

"Fine," the old man murmured.

"Now, I'll give you a shave myself. Or, no"—Dusty took a dollar from his wallet and added some change to it "you can use a haircut, too. This will take care of it. You run along right now, Dad."

"Well"—Mr. Rhodes looked down at the money "hadn't I better wait until the groceries . . . ?"

"I'll take care of them myself. I don't want to go to bed, anyway, until you get back from the barber shop."

"Well, now, there's no need to—"

"I'll be waiting," Dusty said firmly. "I want to be sure you—that they give you a good job."

His father looked at him thoughtfully, the kind of appraising look he had used to give him, back before the trouble had come up, when Dusty's conduct had fallen below standard. Curious, disappointed, but not condemnatory nor surprised.

Dusty stared back at him stolidly.

Mr. Rhodes stood up, shoved the money into the pocket of his stained baggy trousers, and left the house.

The laundry and cleaning men came, then the man from the grocery store. Dusty was in the kitchen, still unpacking and putting away the groceries, when his father returned from the barber shop.

The barber had done his work well. Except for his clothes, Mr. Rhodes might have been Professor Rhodes, principal of Central High School. Dusty was pleased by the transformation, but also annoyed. It confirmed his belief that his father could, if he only chose to, escape the slough of senility into which he seemed to be sinking.

"Well," he said, curtly, "I hope we've got enough here to last a while."

"This meat, Bill"—Mr. Rhodes shook his head. "Why did you get so much? It'll spoil before we can use it."

"I can't be waiting around here every morning while they bring a pound or two, can I?" Dusty rammed the package of meat into the refrigerator. "I can't hang around town in the morning until the stores open. I'm tired when I get off work. I want to get home and get to bed."

"Cornmeal," murmured the old man. "And flour. We never use anything like that, Bill."

"Well"—Dusty's lips pressed together—"I did the best I could. I didn't suppose there'd be any use in asking you what we needed. When I leave it to you, we usually wind up without anything."

"No coffee," said Mr. Rhodes, worriedly. "No fresh milk. Or bread. No—"

"All right!" Dusty yanked a five-dollar bill from his wallet and flung it on the table. "That ought to take care of it! Now, I'm going to bed."

"You don't want something to eat first?"

"I've already eaten. Ate downtown. I—honest to God, Dad, I—"

"You shouldn't have bought so much, Bill." The old man shook his head. "All this stuff, and you eating at home so seldom. You'd better let me do the buying after this."

"How the hell can I? Goddammit, I keep handing money out to you and—"

He broke off, choking down the angry words, ashamed of himself; seeing the futility of talk. His father's mouth had drooped open in that loose, imbecilic way. His eyes were vacantly bewildered. Swiftly, as he always did when the perplexing or troublesome loomed, he had retreated behind the barrier of helplessness.

"Sorry," Dusty said, gruffly. "Have a good day, Dad."

And he entered his bedroom, and closed the door behind him.

Well, hell, he thought, with a kind of sullen remorsefulness. Probably he can't help it; maybe it's the way it has to be. He's had too much to cope with in too short a time. He's all right, as long as things run along smoothly, but the minute any trouble starts . . .

Dusty drew the shades, and turned on the electric fan. He took a few puffs from a cigarette, tapped it out in the ash tray and stretched out on the bed. He turned restlessly, flinging himself around on the rumpled sheets . . . Should have come straight home from work, he thought. Got to sleep while it was still fairly cool. Going to be a scorcher today, and that fan didn't really do any good. Just stirred up the same old air, made a lot of racket. And . . . and how the hell could a guy sleep, anyway? How could you when you were knocking yourself out night after night, and never getting anywhere? When you knew you were never going to get anywhere? His father could go on living for years, and, hell, of course he wanted him to. But—

Dusty groaned, and sat up. He lighted another cigarette, smoked moodily, sitting on the edge of the bed. Dammit— the frown on his pale face deepened—it wasn't fair! It was too much to swallow. There was no excuse for it.

So the old man had lost his job. *And I suppose I didn't lose anything! He's lost his wife. Well, she was my mother, wasn't she? I lost my mother . . .*

Dusty winced, unconsciously. He didn't like to think about his mother. They'd been so close at one time. He could always talk to her, and whatever his problems were she always seemed to understand and sympathize. Then, well, that rumpus over the Free Speech Committee had come up, and Dad had been kicked out of his job. And after that—everything had been different. All her thought, all her sympathy was for his father. To Dusty, she was like— almost—a polite stranger. She wasn't at all concerned about his dropping out of college. College could wait: he was young and his father was old. She took his sacrifices for granted, as something he was obliged to make, a debt that he had to pay. The trouble wasn't his, but it was. He was shut out of it—she drew further and further away from him, drew closer and closer to his father—but he was expected to pay for it. She wouldn't share it with him, this or anything else. Not really share, as she'd used to. He was just a stranger paying off a debt.

. . . It was almost noon before he fell asleep. Five minutes later—what seemed like five minutes—a steady ringing roused him into wakefulness. Automatically, his eyes still closed, he thrust his hand out to the alarm clock. He pressed down on the alarm button—pressed and found it already depressed. He fumbled with it a moment longer, then drowsily opened his eyes.

It was still daylight. Not quite three o'clock. The ringing continued.

He jumped up, ran into the living room and snatched up the telephone.

It was Tolliver, the Manton's superintendent of service.

"Rhodes—Bill?" he said crisply. "Sorry to bother you, but I'll have to ask you to come down to the hotel."

"Come . . . you mean *now?*"

"Sorry, yes. Mr. Steelman wants to see you, and he's not available after five. Come straight to his office, Bill. If anyone gets curious, you can say you came down to see the auditor. A mix-up in your pay or something like that."

"But I don't—is there something wrong? I certainly hope I haven't done—"

Tolliver's laugh was friendly. "Sounds like you've got a guilty conscience. No, it's nothing like that. Nothing that concerns you directly. . . We can expect you right away, Bill?"

"Just as fast as I can get there," Dusty promised.

He was on his way out of the house within ten minutes, still too grumpy with sleep to care much about the reason for the summons . . . That Steelman, he grumbled silently. You'd think he was God instead of just the Manton's manager. *He* "wasn't available" after five, Mr. Steelman wasn't, just couldn't be bothered, no matter what came up. But everyone else had to be available. He could drag *you* out of bed in the middle of the day, and that was perfectly all right.

Dusty found a parking space at the rear of the hotel, and went in the employees' entrance as usual. He rode a service elevator to the second floor, walked on past the auditor's offices and the switchboard room and entered the outer room of the manager's office. The receptionist nodded promptly when he mentioned his name.

"Oh, yes. They're waiting for you. Go right on in."

She gestured toward the door marked PRIVATE. Dusty opened it and went in.

The manager was seated behind his desk, crisp and cool looking in a white linen suit. Tolliver, the superintendent of service, sat a little to one side of him, his fumed-oak chair pulled up at the end of the desk. They were studying some papers when Dusty entered, and they continued to study them for a few moments longer. Then, Steelman murmured something under his breath and Tolliver laughed unctuously, and the two of them looked up.

"Sit down, Bill." Tolliver motioned to a chair. "No, better pull it up here. We'll get this over with as quickly as possible."

Dusty sat down, a faint feeling of nausea in his stomach. It was almost a physical shock to come into this air-conditioned, indirectly-lighted room from the blinding heat outside.

Tolliver went on. "Now this is strictly confidential, Bill. Not a word about it to anyone, you understand? Good. Here's what we want to know. You've been working with Mr. Bascom for about a year. You've been around him more—presumably talked with and observed him more—than any of the rest of us. What can you tell us about him?"

"Tell you?" Dusty smiled puzzledly. "I guess I don't understand what—"

"Put it this way. Has he done or said anything that would lead you to believe he wasn't strictly on the level?"

"Why—why, no, sir." Dusty shook his head. "I mean, well, I don't believe that he has."

"Has he told you anything about his past, what he did before he came here? Any of his experiences, say, at other hotels?"

"No."

"To the best of your knowledge, he's an honest man who

does his work as it should be done?"

"Yes, sir." Dusty looked from Tolliver to Steelman. "I'm not being inquisitive, but maybe if you could tell me what the trouble is I might—"

"Here's the trouble," the manager said crisply. "We've received an anonymous letter about Mr. Bascom. It's not at all specific, doesn't give us any details, but it does indicate that Mr. Bascom's character leaves something to be desired. Ordinarily, we'd pay no attention to such a communication. If one of our other clerks was involved, someone we knew something about—"

"Someone you knew something about?" Dusty frowned. "You mean, you don't know anything about Mr. Bascom?"

"Practically nothing. According to his application blank, he'd always been self-employed, kind of a small-time jobber. He bought novelties and candy and the like from wholesale houses and resold them to retailers. Now, there's nothing wrong with that, of course, but it doesn't tell us much about him. Doesn't give us anything we can check on. And it's the same story with his character references—the director of a YMCA where he lived a few months, the minister of a church he attended. Virtually meaningless. Those people hand out references right and left."

"But"—Dusty spread his hands—"but why did you hire him, then?"

Tolliver laughed wryly. "Doesn't sound much like the Manton, does it, Bill? But you see, Bascom was hired during the war, right back at the beginning of it. We had to take what we could get, and very few questions asked. Afterwards, since he seemed to have worked out very well, we simply let matters ride. We can't very well start questioning him about his background at this late date. Always assuming, of course, that questioning would do any good."

"It wouldn't," said Steelman. "When a man's applying for a job, he tells everything he can that will be a credit to him. No, we have to go on accepting Bascom at his word, which is just about what it boils down to. Or we have to let him go."

"I'd hate to do that," Tolliver said, "with nothing more against him than an anonymous note. I—yes, Bill?"

"I was just going to say that the bonding company must have investigated him. As long as they feel—"

"He isn't bonded. We've never felt it necessary to bond the night clerk. He carries a very small change bank, doesn't handle much cash. He doesn't have access to any valuables. So . . ."

"Let's see," said Steelman. "Do you have many one-shift guests, Rhodes? People who arrive after midnight and leave before seven?"

"Not very many. If you wanted to check the transcript—"

"We already have. I was wondering whether Mr. Bascom ever ordered you to make up those checked-out rooms instead of leaving them for the maids."

"You mean have I helped him steal the price of the room?" Dusty said. "No, sir, I haven't."

"Now, Bill"—Tolliver frowned. "That wasn't Mr. Steelman's question."

"I'm sorry," Dusty said. "No, sir, Mr. Bascom has never told me to do anything like that. He knows that I wouldn't do it if he did ask me. If he was going to pull anything crooked, he'd get rid of me before . . ."

His voice trailed away, leaving the sentence unfinished, Steelman glanced at him shrewdly.

"Go on, Rhodes. He's been riding you, trying to get rid of you?"

"Well," Dusty hesitated. "Yes, sir, he has. But I'm not sure he doesn't mean it for my own good. You see he thinks—he seems to think—that I ought to go back to college."

"Mmm. I wonder," said Steelman. "If he could get another bellboy on the job, work out a deal with him . . . Tolly, do you remember that night team they caught out in Denver a while back? Stealing rent. Refunding—right into their own pockets. Carting out linens and supplies by the armload. God only knows how many thousands of dollars they cleaned up."

"I remember," Tolliver nodded. "But with nothing more against the man than this one letter, which doesn't really tell us anything, I'd be very reluctant to jump to any conclusions. After all, Bascom worked with a number of other bellboys before Bill came here. His work is audited daily, and we run comparison reaudits from month to month. It seems to me that if he was pulling anything, we'd have found out about it in ten years time."

"Perhaps he hasn't pulled anything. Maybe he's just getting ready to."

"Well," said Tolliver. "Maybe."

"I don't like it, Tolly." Steelman's lips thinned fretfully. "A letter like this concerning the one man we know nothing about. If a man's been a crook once—and this indicates that he has—he's very apt to be one again. He feels a sudden pinch, has to get money in a hurry, and he's off to the races."

"Yes, I suppose so," Tolliver nodded. "What about that, Bill? Does Mr. Bascom have any money problems that you know of?"

"No, sir. He's never mentioned any."

"Well, there's still another angle," the manager went on. "Suppose the author of this letter is trying to blackmail Bascom. He doesn't want him dismissed from his job, so he says just enough to disturb us. As he sees it, we'll be impelled to make some mention of the matter and Bascom will be frightened into paying off. Otherwise, there'll be another letter with more details."

Tolliver frowned solemnly. Then, suddenly, his mouth twisted and he bent forward laughing. "Excuse me, John, but—ha, ha, ha—when I try to picture poor old Bascom in the toils of a blackmailer, I— ha, ha—I—"

"Well," Steelman grinned a trifle sheepishly. "Maybe I'd better start reading westerns instead of detective stories. I can't see the prim old boy in the role myself. Seriously, however . . . "

"We've gotten crank letters before, John. It's not unnatural, after all the years he's been with us, that one should eventually crop up about Bascom. If we get another one, we certainly ought to take some action, but I don't see how we can at this point. For the present, we can just keep our eyes and ears open—that means you particularly, Bill—and—"

"What about putting Bascom on a day shift?"

"If you say so, but I wouldn't like to. He doesn't have the zip, the polish for a front-office day job. Aside from that, it takes a long time to break a man in on the night paper work.

Steelman nodded. "All right, Tolly. I'll leave it up to you.
You don't think you should mention the letter to Bascom?
Very casually, of course. If he's on the level, there's no harm
done, and if he isn't, well, it might keep him out of trouble."

"Except with that blackmailer, eh?" Tolliver laughed.
"But I think you may be right, John. Now . . . "

They discussed the matter for a minute or two longer.
Then, Tolliver looked at Dusty and stood up. "There's no
reason to keep Bill around for this, is there? There's nothing
more you have to say to him?"

"Can't think of anything." The manager shook his head.
"Thanks for coming down, Rhodes."

"And remember," Tolliver said, "under your hat, Bill. You
don't know anything about this matter."

"Yes, sir," said Dusty.

. . . Later, when it was too late to do much about it, it
seemed to him that he should have seen the connection
between the letter and Marcia Hillis and Tug Trowbridge
and Bascom . . . and the threat they represented to himself. Later, he did not know he had been so blind as to fail to
see. It was all so simple, simple and deadly. All the parts to
the puzzle had been in his hands, and he had only to look
at them.

That, however, was later. At the time, it was only an
annoyance and one for which there was little excuse. His
sleep had been broken into. He had been dragged downtown on a hot afternoon. And all because some nut, some
guest probably with a hangover grouch, had written an
anonymous note. That was all it amounted to when you got
right down to it. If the hotel had any real doubts about Bascom, he wouldn't have stayed there ten years.

Dusty went home, found that his father had returned
from his stroll or wherever he had been, and went to bed. It
was now nearing six o'clock, but he was too tired and hot to
eat. Too tired to sleep, for that matter. He heard his father
moving about in the kitchen, closing and reclosing the
refrigerator, rattling ice trays, setting a pan on the stove. It
went on and on, it seemed. Interminably. It would—*he
began to drift into sleep*—always go on. The heat and the
noise . . . and . . . and his father. And nothingness.

A vivid image of his mother flashed into his mind, and he

tossed restlessly. The image changed, a line here, a line there, and it was another woman: alluring, youthful, and above all warm and interested . . . and understanding.

He fell asleep, half-frowning, half-smiling.

The night was about average for the Hotel Manton. Bascom seemed about the same as always, with little to say and that cranky and carping. If Tolliver had shown him the letter, and if it meant anything to him, he gave no sign of the fact.

Dusty drove straight home from work. Or, rather, he started to. Halfway there he remembered that his father was to see the optometrist and that he had no clean clothes. Wearily, cursing, he let the car slow. Of course, the cleaning and laundry might get back early today, but it also might not. And now that he'd taken a firm stand with his father, he'd better carry through with it. There was going to be no more of this putting off, letting him go on with his expensive and embarrassing shiftlessness. He'd been told to see the optometrist today, so today it would be.

Dusty drove back to town, eating breakfast while he waited for the stores to open. He bought a pair of summer trousers, a shirt and underwear, and started home again.

Mr. Rhodes was in the kitchen, dabbling ineffectually at the suds-filled sink. He lifted a platter from the dishwater, peering at his son reproachfully as he began to scrub it.

"Had a nice breakfast fixed for you, Bill," he said. "Bacon and eggs and toast, and—"

"Sorry," Dusty said, shortly. "Wash up, and put these on, Dad. I'll drive you down to the optometrist."

"Thought sure you'd be here," the old man went on. "After buying all that stuff yesterday. If you'd told me you were going to be late, I'd—"

"I'm telling you now!" Dusty snapped. "I mean, I'm sorry, but please hurry, Dad. I want to get to sleep. I'll drive you down, and you can come home by yourself."

Mr. Rhodes nodded mildly, and put down the platter.

"This night work, son—do you really think it pays? You don't get your proper rest, and it costs more to—"

"I know. We'll talk about it another time," Dusty cut in. "Now, please hurry, Dad."

He waited in the car while the old man got ready. Impatiently. Trying to stifle his irritation. Probably, he decided, his father was right. He made more money by working nights, but his expenses were higher. There was this car, for example; bus service was slow and irregular late at night, so the car was virtually a necessity. And that was only part of the story. There were usually two sets of meals to fix—or to buy away from home. There was his father, free to do as he chose and always in need of money. Still . . .

Dusty shrugged and shook his head. He wouldn't change jobs for a while, anyway. Not anyway until—and if—he went back to college. He didn't sleep well at night. He hadn't slept well since his mother's death, and, yes, even before that. Of course, it was hard sleeping in the daytime, but that was different. It wasn't like lying alone in the darkness and quiet, thinking and worrying and—and listening.

. . . He drove the old man downtown, and opened the car door for him. Mr. Rhodes started to slide out of the seat, hesitated.

"You know, Bill, we never did get around to talking about my case. I mentioned that letter the other night, and you said—"

"I haven't forgotten," Dusty said. "We'll see about it."

"Well . . . " Mr. Rhodes looked at him thoughtfully, he sighed and put a foot on the sidewalk. "I thought I might go to a show after I get through here, Bill. If that's all right with you."

"You do that," Dusty nodded. "Pick some place with air-conditioning."

"Well, I-I'm not sure that—"

"I am," Dusty said firmly. "You must have enough money, Dad. You couldn't help but have."

"Well . . . well, maybe," the old man mumbled. "I guess I have at that."

He got out and trudged away. Dusty drove home, and went to bed. This was one day, he thought, he'd really get some sleep. He was so tired that . . . that . . .

He was asleep almost the moment that he climbed into bed. An hour later he was aroused by the laundry man.

He put the laundry away, and went back to sleep. Another hour passed—roughly an hour. And the man from the cleaner's came.

This time it was harder returning to sleep. He smoked a couple of cigarettes, got a drink of water, tossed and turned restlessly on the bedclothes. Finally, at long last, he drifted off into unconsciousness. And the phone rang.

He tried to ignore it, to pretend that it was not ringing. It rang on and on, refusing to be denied. Cursing, Dusty flung himself out of bed and answered it.

"Mr. Rhodes? Hope I didn't interrupt anything, but your father said I was to be sure to . . . "

It was the optometrist.

Dusty learned the amount of his bill, muttered a goodbye and slammed the phone back in its cradle. He returned to bed, but now, of course, sleep was impossible. His eyes kept popping open. His head throbbed with a surly, sullen anger. Unreasoning, focusing gradually on just one object . . . Why the hell did *he* have to go to a show today? Why couldn't *he* ever do anything except make a damned nuisance of himself? All *he* thought of was his own comfort, his own welfare. Lying and sponging to get money for those—

Abruptly, Dusty got up. Sullenly ashamed, vaguely alarmed. He didn't really feel that way about his father. He couldn't be blamed much if he did, but he didn't. He didn't feel at all that way. He was just grouchy with the heat and work and not being able to sleep.

There was still some coffee on the stove. He drank a cup, smoking a cigarette with it, and went into the bathroom. Today was as good a time as any to see those lawyers. A good time to get it over with, since he couldn't sleep. He came out of the bathroom, dressed and headed for town.

. . . The building was an old faded-brick walkup, squatting almost directly across the street from the county courthouse. Dusty climbed the worn stairs to the second floor, and proceeded past a series of doors with the legend:

McTeague & Kossmeyer

Attorneys at Law
Entrance 200

Room 200 was at the end of the corridor, uncarpeted,
high-ceilinged, barren of everything—it seemed to Dusty—
except spitoons and people. A low wooden rail with a
swinging gate enclosed one corner of the room. Dusty
made his way to the barrier, and gave his name to a gray-
ing, harried-looking woman.

"McTeague?" she said. "Something personal? You a
friend of his? Well, you don't see Mac then. Kossy does all
the seeing in this firm."

"Well . . . " Dusty hesitated. He didn't want to see
Kossmeyer—"Caustic" Kossmeyer, as the newspapers
called him. From what he had observed of the attorney, it
would not be easy to say the things to him that he had come
to say.

"Well," the woman said. "Kossmeyer?"

"You're sure I can't—?"

"Kossmeyer," she said grimly. With finality. And jabbed a
plug into her switchboard. "Now sit down and stay put,
will you? Don't go wandering off someplace where I can't
find you."

She kept her eyes on him until he sat down—on a bench
between a middle-aged Mexican in soiled khakis and a
middle-aged matron in crisp cretonne. Dusty started to
light a cigarette, then noting the sidelong glance the matron
gave him, dropped it into one of the ubiquitous spittoons.
Uncomfortably, he looked around the room.

A young, scared-looking couple sat in one of the windows, holding hands. A few feet away from them, a
paunchy man in an expensive suit talked earnestly to a bos-
omy, flashily dressed blonde. Two men with zoot coats and
snapbrimmed hats were playing the match game. Three
Negroes, obviously mother, father and son, huddled in a
corner and conversed in whispers . . . It was as though a
cross-section of the city's population had been swept up
and set down in the room.

Dusty stood up, casually. The receptionist wasn't looking
at him. He'd just saunter on out. Tomorrow he'd write a
letter to the firm. A letter would do just as well as a per-

sonal talk—almost as well, anyway—and . . .

The door inside the barrier opened, and Kossmeyer came out. Rather, he lunged out, pushing a sharp-faced oldish young man ahead of him. His voice rasped stridently through the suddenly stilled room.

"All right," he was saying. "Suit yourself. Be your own lawyer. But don't come crying to me afterwards. You want to go to the jug, it's your funeral, but I ain't sending any flowers."

"Now, look, Kossy"—the man's eyes darted around the room. "I didn't mean—"

"You look," said Kossmeyer. "You ever see yourself in a mirror? Well, take a good gander . . . "

Dusty watched, fascinated.

Kossmeyer didn't look anything like the other man; he was barely five feet tall and he couldn't have weighed more than a hundred pounds. But now, despite their facial and physical dissimilarity, he looked strikingly like him. In an instant, he had made himself into a hideous caricature of the other. His eyes had become shifting and beady, his face sinisterly slack-jawed. He had caved in his chest, simultaneously squaring his shoulders so that his elbows were forced out from his sides. His pants were drawn high beneath his armpits. He wore no coat, but he seemed to, a coat that hung almost to the knees like the other man's. Eyes darting he slowly revolved, not moving a muscle of his dead-pan face . . .

He was preposterous. Preposterous yet somehow frightening. A cartoon labelled CRIME. And, then, suddenly, he was himself again.

"You see, Ace? You got three strikes called the minute they look at you. Just handing it to 'em straight ain't good enough. We got to knock 'em over, know what I mean? Pile it around 'em so high they can't see over it."

The man nodded. "You got me sold. Now, how about—"

"Beat it. Come back tomorrow." Kossmeyer gave him a shove through the gate, and bent over the receptionist. He said, "Yeah? Where?" and glanced up. Then Dusty heard him say, "Oh . . . the son . . . junior . . . "

And the next instant he was out of the enclosure and gripping Dusty's hand.

"Glad to see you, Rhodes, Bill . . . No, I bet they call you Dusty, don't they? Come on in."

Dusty hung back. Or tried to. "I—it's nothing important, Mr. Kossmeyer. I can come back some other—"

"Nonsense." The attorney propelled him through the throng. "Been hoping you'd drop in. Let's see, you're over at the Manton, right? Nice people. Done a little work for them myself. How's your father? How you like this weather? What . . . ?"

Talking rapidly, answering his own questions, he ushered Dusty into his office and slammed the door.

Except for the bookcases, the room was practically as barren as the one outside. Kossmeyer waved Dusty to a chair, and perched on the desk in front of him.

"Glad you came in," he repeated. "Wanted to ask you, but I knew you worked nights. How about a drink? You look kind of tired."

"Thanks. I don't drink," Dusty said.

"Yeah? Well I was saying— I'm damned glad you came in. I got a pretty good idea how you feel, Dusty. We've been on this thing about a year now, and we seem to be getting nowhere fast. Your father still out of a job. You stuck with a lot of expenses. You're asking yourself, what the hell, and I don't blame—"

"About that"—Dusty cleared his throat. "About the expenses, Mr. Kossmeyer. I'm afraid I can't—I mean, it seems to me that—"

"Sure." The little man nodded vigorously. "They've been high. Just the costs alone on a deal like this can hit a guy pretty hard. I—" he paused. "You know that's all we've taken, don't you? Just the actual expense of filing briefs and serving papers, and so on."

"Well, no," Dusty said. "I didn't know it. But—"

"But it's still too much," Kossmeyer interrupted. "Anything's too much when it ain't buying anything. But that's just the way it looks to you, y'know, Dusty? It's just the way it looks from the outside. Actually, we're making a lot of headway. We've been pouring in the nickels, and now we're just about to hit the jackpot. I—"

"Mr. Kossmeyer," said Dusty, "I want you to drop the case."

"Huh-uh. No, you don't," the lawyer said. "You just think you do. Like I've been telling you, kid, we're just about to pick up the marbles. Give me two or three more months, and—"

"It won't do any good if Dad does win. He's not going to be able to go back to his job. He's not—well, he's just not himself any more."

"Who the hell is?" Kossmeyer shrugged. "But I know what you mean, Dusty. I've seen him myself, y'know. This knocked the props out from under him, and he's still going around in a daze. I'd say the best way to snap him out of it is to—"

"He's not physically well either. He's—"

"Sure, he's not," Kossmeyer agreed. "A man's sick, he's sick all over."

"I want you to drop it," Dusty said stubbornly. "Winning the case won't really change anything. People will go right on thinking that—what they've been thinking. It would be impossible for him to work."

"Yeah, but, kid . . . " Kossmeyer paused, a puzzled frown on his small, sharp-featured face. "Let me see if I got you right, Dusty. We're supposed to have free speech in this country; it's guaranteed by the constitution. So a man does something in support of that guarantee, and a bunch of know-nothings and professional patriots do a job on him. He's right and they're as wrong as teeth in a turkey, but he's supposed to take it. Just crawl in a hole and stay there. Don't give 'em no trouble, so they can go on and do the same kind of job on another guy. Is that what you mean?"

"I'm sorry," Dusty said doggedly. "I can't help it that things are the way they are. It's not right, of course, but—"

"I think you're low-pricing your dad," Kossmeyer said. "He thought enough of this issue to go to bat on it. I don't see him running for the dugout just because they're tossing pop bottles. If he gets his job back—*when* he gets it back, I should say—he won't let 'em smoke him out. He'll be right in there pitching a long time after these bastards are ducking for cover themselves."

He nodded firmly. Dusty shook his head. "I don't think he felt that way. I mean, well, like he was fighting for something. I doubt that he even knew what he was signing. Someone handed him a petition and he just . . . "

"Yeah?" Kossmeyer waited. "Why didn't he say so, then? That it was all a misunderstanding? That would have let him off the hook."

"Well," Dusty hesitated. "I . . . he probably thought they wouldn't believe him."

"I see," said Kossmeyer. "Well, possibly you're right. After all, if a son doesn't know his father, who does?"

He stared at Dusty blandly, his bright black eyes friendly and guileless. And yet there was something about him, there had been something for several minutes now, that was vaguely disturbing. He was like some small deadly bird, coaxing a clumsy prey within striking distance.

Dusty took out his cigarettes, fumbled one from the package. Instantly, Kossmeyer was holding a match for him.

"Had a pretty rough time of it, haven't you, kid? Losing out on your schooling. Losing your mother. Working and trying to take care of a sick old man at the same time."

"I don't mind," Dusty said. "I'm glad to do what I can."

"Sure, you are, but it's plenty tough just the same. Well, I thought we'd gone pretty easy with you on money, but maybe we can make it a little lighter still. That's your only objection to going on with the case, isn't it? The expense. If we can take care of that, you'd just as soon we went ahead."

"Well, I—I wouldn't want you to—"

"We'll work something out," Kossmeyer said. "Maybe—y'know, it's just possible we can get by without any more expenses. If I can get your father to cooperate."

"If . . . ?" Dusty's head was beginning to ache. "I don't understand."

"You gave me an idea a minute ago. About your father signing that petition without knowing what he was doing. Now, that might be pretty hard for people to swallow, particularly at this late date. And I kind of think he wouldn't want to make such an admission, anyway. If he wasn't any brighter than that, he shouldn't have been holding the job he was in . . . "

"But what—"

"That petition was floating around everywhere. Different

copies of it. Maybe someone signed your dad's name to it. You . . . Here! You're about to burn your fingers, kid."

Kossmeyer reached behind him and procured an ashtray. He extended it in a lean, steady hand.

Dusty ground out his cigarette. "Why would anyone sign his name?"

"Some joker maybe. Some guy who wanted to get him into trouble."

"But why wouldn't Dad have said so if—"

"We-el"—Kossmeyer pursed his lips—"now, that's a question, ain't it? Ordinarily, I'd say he was standing on the principle of the thing. He had a right to sign it, and regardless of whether he did or not isn't important. It's the principle involved, not the physical action itself. But you say he doesn't feel that way, so— That *is* what you said, isn't it?—so I guess he must have another reason."

He continued to stare at Dusty, frowning thoughtfully, interested and sympathetic: a man helping a friend with a puzzling problem. He waited, watched and waited, and Dusty could only look back at him wordlessly, his throat dry, a slow hot flush creeping over his face. The silence mounted. It became unbearable.

And then Kossmeyer shrugged, and grinned deprecatingly. "Listen to me rave, huh? Who the hell would forge your old man's signature? It don't make sense any way you look at it. All your dad would have to do is call in a handwriting expert, and he'd be in the clear like that."

He snapped his fingers, demonstrating. He slid off the desk, and held out his hand. "Don't want to rush you off, kid, but I got a lot of people waiting and . . . "

"I've got to run along, anyway." Dusty stood up hastily. "I'll—thanks very much for seeing me, and—"

It wasn't what he wanted to say. He hadn't said anything he'd wanted to say. He'd gotten all twisted around, and all he could think of now was release. All he wanted now was to escape from this friendly, helpful and terrifying little man.

"I'll—I hope I see you again," he mumbled weakly.

"Sure you will." Kossmeyer gave him a hearty clap on the back. "Any old time, kid. If it ain't convenient for you to come in, I'll look you up."

He held the door open, beaming, ushered Dusty through it. He shook hands again. "Yes, sir," he said. "I'll keep in touch. You can depend on it, Dusty."

As it often did, after a scorching day, the night brought rain. It had started a few minutes before Dusty came to work; now, at three in the morning, it had settled down to a slow steady drizzle.

It was a quiet shift. No guests had come in on the late train, and there had been hardly a dozen room calls thus far. He and Bascom were practically through with their paper work; at least, there was little remaining that he could help with. Lounging at the side of the door of the lobby, he drank in the wonderfully cool clean air, watching the curtain of rain flow endlessly into the oily black pavement.

He was feeling good, all things considered, considering that he had had almost no sleep. It was cool, and Kossmeyer hadn't guessed anything—what the hell was there for him to guess, anyway?—and Bascom was being decent for a change. Bascom had been taking a lot out of him, Dusty decided. You were bound to be nervous and depressed when you had some guy riding you night after night.

Dusty flipped his cigarette into the street, and went back into the lobby. Bascom called to him pleasantly from the cashier's cage.

"How does it look, Bill? Still coming down pretty hard?"

"Not too bad. You can make it all right if you take an umbrella."

"Good. Think I'll go get a bite to eat, then."

Dusty went behind the desk. Bascom came out of the cashier's cage, locked the door behind him and got an umbrella. He opened the door at the rear of the keyrack, and emerged into the lobby.

"Well"—his voice was casual; he spoke almost over his shoulder—"I guess you're not going to go back to college?"

"I'm still thinking about it," Dusty said. "I want to, but it'll take time to work it out."

"I see," Bascom noded. "At any rate, I don't suppose you could go back before the fall term."

"No, sir. Not very well."

"I'll be back in a few minutes," Bascom said. "You know where to reach me if anything comes up."

He went out the side door, raising the umbrella as he stepped under the marquee. Dusty leaned his elbows on the marble desk top, and let his eyes wander around the lobby. He yawned pleasurably. A good night, any way you looked at it. Bascom, the weather, money-wise. Tug Trowbridge had given him a ten-dollar tip. If he didn't make another nickel between now and quitting time, he'd still have a good shift.

At his elbow, the bell captain's phone rang suddenly. Dusty jumped, startled, then picked up the receiver.

It was her, Marcia Hillis. He recognized her voice instantly, and she recognized his.

"Dusty? Can you bring me some stationery?"

"Yes, ma'am. Right away, Miss—I mean, I can bring them in a few minutes, Miss Hillis. The room clerk's gone out to eat, and I have to watch the desk."

"Oh? Are you afraid it will run away?"

"No, ma'am, I—"

She laughed softly. "I was teasing. . . . As soon as you can, then."

"Yes, ma'am."

He hung the receiver up clumsily. Opening a drawer, he took out a stack of stationery, small and typewriter size, and laid it on the counter. He went behind the keyrack to the lavatory and combed his hair. He came out front again, and looked at the clock. Bascom had been gone . . . well, he'd been gone long enough. Should be back any minute. He looked at the stack of stationery, shook his head judiciously, and returned two thirds of it to the drawer.

Something in the action stirred his memory. Or, perhaps, it was the other way around: memory, a recollection, brought about the action. Something the superintendent of service had lectured him about at the time of his employment.

" . . . *Very careful about waste, Bill. Lights not in use, leaky water taps, two trips with the elevator when one might suffice, more soap and towels and stationery than a guest can legitimately use. Little things . . . but they aren't little when you multiply them by several hundred. It's those little things that count. They make the difference between profit and loss . . . "*

Dusty glanced at the clock again. For no reason that he could think of, merely to kill time, he walked up the aisle to the room rack. There was nothing to be learned there, of course. She was just another one of hundreds of small white slips . . . a capital-lettered composite name, place of residence, rate and date. . . . He returned to the bell captain's section, drummed nervously on the neat stack of stationery.

He picked up the outside phone, dialed the first two numbers of the lunch room, and replaced the receiver. This wasn't important enough to have Bascom come rushing back. If she waited until this time of night to write letters, she could wait a little longer. That's the way Bascom would look at it. That was the way he looked at it. She was just another guest, good for a two-bit tip, perhaps. So what was the hurry?

Dusty leaned over the counter, and looked up the expanse of lobby to the front entrance. He went out the door and waited in front of the counter.

Stationery at three in the morning. Not usual, but it wasn't extraordinary either. A guest couldn't sleep, so to pass the time, he or she wrote letters. It happened. Every few nights or so there'd be a room call for stationery. As for the way she'd talked over the phone, the way she'd acted that first night . . .

Well . . .

He shrugged and ended the silent argument. Why kid himself? She'd been interested in him from the beginning. Now, she'd worked herself up to the point of doing a little playing. And so long as she wasn't a spotter—and she wasn't—so long as he let her take all the initiative and he damned well would—it would be okay. No trouble. Not a chance of trouble. He'd never done anything like this before, and he never would again. Just this once.

Bascom came in the front door. Dusty signaled to him, jabbing a finger into the air. The room clerk nodded, and

Dusty picked up the stationery and trotted off to the elevator.

At the tenth floor, he opened the door of the car and latched it back with a hook. He started down the long semidark corridor. There was a low whistle from behind him, then a:

"Hey, Dusty!"

Dusty turned. It was Tug Trowbridge, standing in the door of his suite in undershirt and trousers. Two men— the two he had met a few nights before—were with him.

"In a big hurry? How about running my friends downstairs?"

"Well"—Dusty hesitated—"yes, sir," he said. "Glad to." It had to be done. He couldn't leave them waiting indefinitely for an elevator.

He took them downstairs, said good night and went back to the tenth floor. He latched the door back quietly, and started down the hall again.

Slowly, then more slowly.

Now that he was here, rounding the corner of the corridor, approaching her door, standing in front of it—now, his nervousness, his sense of caution, returned. An uneasy premonition stirred in him, a feeling that once before he had done something like this with terrifying, soul-sickening results. There had been another woman, one who like this one was all woman, and he—

He shook himself, driving the memory deep down into its secret hiding place. It had never happened, nothing like this. There had been no other woman.

He raised his hand, tapped lightly on the door. He heard a soft, rustling sound, then, dimly, "Dusty?"

"Yes."

"Come in."

He went in, let the door click shut behind him. He stood there a moment, his eyes still full of the light outside, seeing nothing in the pitch black darkness. His hand unclasped, and the stationery drifted to the floor.

She laughed softly. She murmured . . . a question, an invitation. He felt his way forward slowly, guided by the sound of her voice.

His knee bumped against the bed. A hand reached up out

of the darkness. He sat down on the edge of the bed, and her arms fastened around his neck.

There was one savagely delightful moment as his mouth found hers, as he felt the cool-warm nakedness of her breasts. Then, suddenly, he was sick, shivering with sickness and fear. It was all wrong. It wasn't like it should have been.

Her mouth was covered with lipstick. He could taste its ugly flatness in his own mouth, feel the sticky smears upon his face and neck. And she wasn't naked. Only part of her was nude, and there the nakedness was not complete. It was as though her night clothes had been torn. It—

She didn't speak. She was still clinging to him, smearing him, digging her nails into his face. She didn't speak, but there was a voice:

"Y-you filthy, sneaking little bastard! Yes, bastard, do you hear? We got you out of a foundling asylum! And God curse the day we . . . No, I won't tell him. I won't do that to him. But if you ever—"

He was almost motionless for a moment, paralyzed by the unbearable voice. But it had never happened. It was only a bad dream. And this . . .

There was a roll of thunder. The drawn curtains whipped back in a sudden gust of wind, and lightning illuminated the room just for a second, but that was long enough for him to see:

The over-turned chairs. The upset lamp. The deliberate disorder. The night-gown, half ripped from her body. And the smeared red mouth, opened to scream. He hit her as hard as he could.

The next thirty minutes was a nightmare. A confused and hideous dream, the incidents of which piled terrifyingly, bewilderingly, one atop another. He was bent over her—pleading and apologizing—hysterically trying to bring her back to consciousness. Then, he was leaving her room, running blindly down the hall, bursting into Tug

Trowbridge's suite. And Tug was gripping him by the shoulders, slapping him across the face, forcing him into a semi-calm coherence . . . *"So okay, kid. I'll try and square the dame some way. Now straighten up and beat it back downstairs. Before old Bascom sends out an alarm for you."*

He was washing his face, combing his hair, under Tug's supervision. He was in the elevator, then crossing a seemingly endless expanse of the lobby. With Bascom's eyes on him every step of the way. And at last—at last, immediately—he was facing Bascom across the marble counter.

Trying to explain the inexplicable.

"Bill! Answer me, Bill!"

"Y-yes, sir . . . ?"

"What took you so long? What have you been doing up there in Miss Hillis' room?"

"I—I—"

It made no impression on him at the time: the fact that, illogically, Bascom knew where he had been. He was still too frightened, too conscience-stricken, to raise even a silent question.

"Bill!"

"N-nothing, sir. The—the window in her room was stuck. I had to pry it open for her. P-prop it open."

"And that took you thirty minutes? Nonsense! What were you doing up there? What have you done to—to—"

Bascom's voice trailed away. Eyes fastened on Dusty's face, he picked up the telephone. Gave a room number to the operator.

Dusty would have run, then. He would have, but his legs refused to obey the frantic signaling of his mind. He could only stand, paralyzed, wait and listen as Bascom spoke into the phone.

" . . . uh, Miss Hillis? This is the night clerk. The bellboy tells me that you were having some trouble—that there was some trouble with your window, and . . . I see. You're all right—I mean, everything is taken care of, then? Thank you very much, and I hope I haven't disturbed you."

He hung up the phone. Incredibly, he hung it up . . . without summoning the police or the house detective. And, seemingly, the nightmare began to draw to a close.

Dusty could breathe again. He could talk—and think—again.

Tug had squared the dame some way. He'd bought her off. Or, more likely, he'd frightened her away from whatever stunt she'd been attempting. Probably he'd been there in the room with her when Bascom called. Letting her know—making her believe—that she'd get her teeth slapped out if she pulled anything funny.

At any rate, everything was all right. A miracle had happened, and he was too grateful to inquire as to its creation or authenticity.

"I told you," he said—he heard himself saying. "What the hell did you think I was doing?"

Bascom frowned at him puzzledly. He gave him a long, level look, and at last turned back to his work on the transcript sheets.

"I'll tell you what I think," he said. "What I've been thinking for quite a while. You don't belong here in this job. Sooner or later, if you stay on, you'll find yourself in very serious trouble."

Dusty laughed. Almost steadily. "What have you got it in for me about, anyway? I can't turn around any more without you making a production out of it."

"Come around the desk," said Bascom. "Give me some help. Do a little something to earn your pay."

"Sure," Dusty grinned. "Why not?"

He and the clerk finished the few remaining two man chores. Then, Bascom retired to the cashier's cage, and Dusty sauntered back to the bell-captain's area. Elbows propped on the marble counter, he wondered—without really caring—how Tug had managed to square Miss Marcia Hillis, of Dallas, Tex.

A little slapping around, he supposed, not enough to mark her up, but more than enough to scare hell out of her. She hadn't counted on his having a friend like Tug. She'd framed him into a case of seeming attempted rape, the objective a hefty lawsuit against the hotel. But now that she'd seen what she was up against, that the only thing she was likely to collect was a broken neck . . .

Dusty frowned, still not actually caring or worrying about her, but continuing to wonder. He'd have sworn that she wasn't a shakedown artist. How could he have been so wrong? And if she was one—*since* she was one—why had she waited so long to pull this rape setup?

A dame as smart as she seemed to be would have made the try right away. She'd have known that the hotel might become suspicious, decide that her room was subject to "previous reservation" and that, regrettably, no others were available.

She should have know that. Anyone who knew anything at all about hotels, *had* to know it. And yet . . . Dusty's face cleared, and he smiled almost pityingly. Despite the ordeal she'd put him through, he felt a little sorry for her.

She *didn't* know anything about hotels: that was the answer to the riddle. She was a swell-looking babe, and doubtless smart enough in other respects, but what she didn't know about hotels was everything. As little as she knew about the rackets.

He'd been right about her. She wasn't a shakedown operator. This was her first attempt. She'd been rocking along somewhere, respectably enough, and then she'd gotten this big idea—one she thought was completely original. So she'd gone to work on it. And made every blunder in the book.

The Manton itself had been blunder number one. A professional would have chosen a really big house with heavy turnover in personnel and guests. Then, there was error number two—a thing to make a real pro wince. That was her biggest bonehead, checking in in the middle of the night, without a reservation for God's sake! And demanding a low-priced room! And making a play, arousing the suspicions of an employee, before she was ready to carry through with it. . . .

One mistake after another. In a way, her many and incredible blunders had protected her. Ignorance had masqueraded as innocence, and while he had been disturbed by her, he had had no strong suspicions.

Well . . . Dusty sighed regretfully. She wasn't the only one who'd been stupid. If he'd seen the simple truth sooner, he could have avoided tonight's terrifying experience. Replaced it with one exceedingly more pleasant. He could have said, Look, honey. You're trying this in the wrong place and on the wrong guy . . . And doubtless she would have been grateful. Very grateful.

As things stood now—well, just where did things stand now? Covertly, he glanced down the long aisle toward Bascom, hesitated, then sighed again. The clerk was already suspicious. Aside from that, a call or a visit to her room was out of the question. She'd be frightened and angry, afraid of and ready to repel any overtures he might make. Also, Tug might still be with her . . . and so occupied as to make him resent an intrusion. That would be like Tug. She had made trouble for the big man; in a word, she owed him something. And he would collect as a matter of course.

Dusty wished he could get her out of his mind. He wished he could feel more relieved, grateful, for escaping from what had seemed an inescapable mess. But as the long night drew to a close, he felt only one thing: a sense of irreplaceable loss. He had lost her *again*. For the second time, he had lost the only woman in the world.

The vanguard of the day shift began to arrive. The first elevator boy went to work, the first mezzanine maid, the first lobby attendant. The head baggage-porter retrieved the checkroom key, unlocked it under the drowsy gaze of a black-shirted subordinate.

As dawn spread into daylight, Dusty was forced out of his reverie. With the calls piling on top of each other he was kept too busy to think about her.

He raced up and down on the service elevator, *de rigueur*, when in use, for the hotel's employees. He raced up and down the long, deeply carpeted hallways. Tapping on doors. Delivering cigarettes and morning papers and toilet articles and a dozen-odd things. Everything moved in a blur of automatic action. There were no people, only room numbers. And the numbers themselves soon lost meaning. They were connected with the transitory moment's errand, and beyond that they had no existence.

. . . He said, "Thank you, very much, sir," and pocketed a quarter tip. He rounded the corner of the corridor, moving at a fast trot.

He looked up, just in time to keep from piling into them.

The baggage porter was in the lead, her overnight case under one arm, her hatbox and suitcase in his hands. Sauntering along behind him was one of Tug's men, and at the rear of the procession was another. She was walking between the two. Knotted at the back of her head were the cords of a heavy black veil.

Dusty gulped. He turned and darted back around the corner. He couldn't say why the scene was such a shock to him, why it sent waves of sickness through his brain. Because, naturally, he should have expected something like this. Tug would feel that he had to get her out of the hotel. Nothing less would be safe—absolutely safe—and Tug was not the kind to take unnecessary chances. So . . . so there was nothing wrong. Tug, or, rather, Tug's boys would see that she checked out. They'd slip her a little money and load her on a train, and—and that was all they would do. Just enough to insure Tug's safety and his, Dusty's, own.

Everything was as it should be, then. As he should have expected it to be. But still he was sick, and getting sicker by the moment. It was as though he'd witnessed a death procession, a criminal being led to the execution chamber.

He ran down the service stairs to the next landing. He raced down that corridor, and around to the service elevator. Why, he couldn't have said, because certainly he couldn't interfere. It would be his own neck if he did, and . . . and why should he, anyway?

Why, he demanded furiously. She tried to get me, didn't she? They won't do anything to her, but why should I care if they did?

The sickness mounted. It disintegrated suddenly, still in him but spread through his body, no longer a compact, centralized force. And mixing with it, adulterating it, was a strange feeling of pride. Tug Trowbridge. He and Tug. She'd stepped on Dusty's toes, and now, by God, she was learning a lesson. They were showing her, her and the Manton and the rest of the world. She had everything on her side, all the forces of law and order. And against him and Tug, they didn't mean a thing. She was being kidnaped in broad daylight from one of the biggest hotels in town.

They were bolder than the others, see? They could think faster than the others. Sure, everyone knew who Tug's boys were, but the boys weren't with her, understand? They just happened to be around when she decided to check out.

They made her call for a porter. Then, they set her baggage out in the hall, and told her to wait there until the porter arrived. And when he did, well, they were just down the hall a few steps, just coming out of another room — it appeared. And very casually, oh, so innocently, they all headed for the elevator together. True, one got ahead of the other, but what of it? Doubtless the second guy had had to pause to tie a shoelace.

Dusty stepped off the elevator, hurried toward the entrance to the lobby. He was panting unconsciously; the pounding of his heart grew wilder and wilder. The next step, now—how would he and Tug manage that! She'd have to pay her own bill. She'd have to leave the hotel alone. They wouldn't dare let her, but they'd have to. God, what else could they do? And once she got out on the street—or, Christ, even before she got to the street even here in the lobby . . . !

They couldn't hold a gun in her back down here. They couldn't follow her right up to the cashier's cage, wait until she paid her bill, and then march her out to the street. They couldn't, but they had to! They had to without letting anyone know they were doing it. And how the hell could they manage that?

Blindly, Dusty entered the lobby. The swelling pride was gone, now; disintegrated as suddenly as the sickness. And the sickness was coagulating and mounting again, taking charge of his every fiber and cell.

He and Tug, rather, Tug and his boys would never get away with it. They were a bunch of stupid stumblebums, and they'd got him in twice the mess he'd already been in, and—

The four were just emerging from the elevator. They passed within inches of him as he paused near the check stand, too stricken to proceed into the lobby proper. Blinded, choking with sickness and terror.

Hell, why had they had to do it like this? Why try to do it so damned right that it was bound to be wrong? They shouldn't have bothered with her baggage or her bill. Just left the bags in her room, and let the bill go unpaid. Of course, that would cause troublesome inquiries eventually. The hotel would chalk her up as a skip, and her name and description would be circularized in every hotel in the country. Her baggage would be opened and examined. Her hometown police would be notified. And if it appeared that she was a responsible person—that she'd simply dropped out of sight in this city—well, it could be tough for anyone who'd had contact with her. But that would be better than this, wouldn't it? You'd stand a chance that way, and this way there was no chance. You were licked before you started.

. . . The baggage porter was heading toward the taxi entrance. She was proceeding up the lobby toward the cashier's cage. Quite alone, now, for the two men had dropped well behind. They had paused to talk, casually, letting her go on alone. Leaving her to scream or run—to appeal to that blurred figure who stood in front of the cashier's cage.

She went forward slowly, stiffly, like a person walking in her sleep. She was almost there, almost safe, completely beyond the reach of her guards.

Why doesn't she do it? Dusty though angrily. *Just do it and get it all over with.*

A voice rang in his ears, booming, familiar. Tug Trowbridge's confident, ever-cheerful bellow. It penetrated the chaos of Dusty's mind, clearing his terror-blurred vision.

Tug. It was he who stood at the cashier's window. Now, he stepped back politely, making room for the woman, and called again to the two men:

"Hey, you guys! Been waiting for you."

They looked up. They allowed themselves to discover him. They joined him.

The three of them stood in a semi-circle, only a few feet withdrawn from the cashier's cage. Ringing her in (although no one would have suspected it), while they held inaudible but patently earnest conversation.

She finished paying her bill. She picked up her change awkwardly, and turned away from the wicket. And Tug put an end to the conversation with another bellow.

"Well, that's that," he announced to the lobby at large. "We'll get busy on it right way, and—hey, you lug! Get out of the lady's way, will you?"

The man addressed stepped out of the "lady's" way. They all stepped out of her way, gesturing and murmuring politely.

She stood motionless for a moment Then, head bowed a little, she started toward the taxi entrance. The three men fell in behind her.

They followed her down the steps, and out to the street. They lingered on the walk while she tipped and dismissed the porter. Then . . .

Heart pounding with relief, his exultation growing again, Dusty moved out into the lobby at last. He stepped over to the front post, with its direct view of the sidewalk, and watched this final and most important step.

Not that he doubted its success. He and Tug had swung the deal this far, and they could swing this. But just how— *how* was something he hadn't thought through. It was a fearful stumbling block which only Tug knew how to surmount.

She had a cab waiting. It was her cab, called for her by the porter, and her baggage was loaded into it. And if they tried to pile in with her . . .

They *did* pile in with her. They almost shoved her inside and climbed in themselves. The door slammed, and the plain black vehicle pulled away from the curb, disappeared in the traffic. And Dusty was puzzled for a moment, but only a moment.

Naturally, the driver hadn't squawked. He was one of Tug's boys. He'd been posted at the entrance in advance, and with a cab already there, why should the porter have called another one?

Dusty grinned. He turned back around, grinning, and looked straight into Bascom's eyes.

His throat went suddenly dry; his contorted lips felt as stiff as stone. For, obviously, Bascom knew. He had seen it all, and he knew what it was all about. He didn't know why it had happened, perhaps, but he knew what had happened. The fact of his knowledge was spread like a picture over his pale, old face.

"W-well?" Dusty said. And then louder, boldly, "Well?" for something else was spread over the room clerk's face: Terror and sickness far greater than he, Dusty, had known that night.

"Bill . . ." Bascom's voice was quaveringly servile. "I —

you don't hold any grudge against me, do you, Bill? I know
I may have appeared to give you a pretty rough time, but it
was only because I—"

"Yeah?" Dusty's grin was back. "What are you driving at?"

"I don't want anyone else to suffer for it, Bill. For the way
you might feel about me. You wouldn't do that, would you?
You wouldn't try to put me on a spot by—by—" Dusty's
grin widened. Bascom was scared out of his wits, and he
damned well should be. The woman was his responsibility.
He'd been flagrantly stupid in ever letting her have a room.
Now, if something happened to her—if, through her, the
hotel became involved in a scandal—Bascom's name would
be mud.

Dusty stared at the clerk. He shrugged contemptuously.
"I don't know what you're talking about," he said.

"Please, Bill. I know how you feel about me, but—"

"Do you? Well, that's good."

The old man's eyes blazed. Then all the fire went out of
them, leaving nothing but lifeless ashes.

"I've got some calls here for you, Bill. I took care of them
for you while you were gone."

"Well," said Dusty, ironically. "Well, well. Now, that was
certainly thoughtful of you, *Mister* Bascom!"

He shuffled through the call slips, then glanced at the
lobby clock. Yawning, he flicked the slips with a finger, scat-
tering them over the counter, sending some of them down
behind the counter. "Save them for the day shift," he said.
"I'm about due to knock off."

The exalted mood lasted until he reached home. It began
to fade as he ascended the steps of the shabby old
house. After five minutes with his father it was gone completely.

Dusty could not say what it was about the old man that
wrought such a sudden and sharp change in his mood. Perhaps, he admitted glumly, a little guiltily, there was really
nothing. Mr. Rhodes had made himself fairly presentable.

He looked and talked almost as well as he had in the old days, and for once—for once!—he did not need money. Still, there he was; that he *was* at all was the trouble. Someone who provided nothing, yet had to be provided for. Someone to be accounted to. Someone who served as a reminder of things that were best forgotten.

Feeling ashamed, Dusty gave the old man five dollars. ("Spend it on anything you want to, Dad.") But the gift, admittedly made for his own sake and not his father's, did nothing to dispel the pangs of conscience. He retired to his room, writhing inwardly, gripped in the black coils of an almost unbearable depression.

He undressed quietly. He turned on the electric fan, and lay back on the bed. He lighted a cigarette . . . and as the minutes ticked by he continued to light them. One from the butt of another.

The humid summer air moved back and forth across his body. It did not actually cool, but it dried. And always there was more to dry. He thought, forcing himself to think back to the beginning—the only beginning he was aware of—and the perspiration rolled out of his pores, dried under the lazy exhalations of the fan.

. . . Yes, he remembered. He had been five at the time of the adoption. He knew that they were not actually his parents. But it had been an easy thing to forget. She made it easy, starved as she was for the motherhood she could not naturally achieve.

He was her own-est, dearest baby, Mama's very own darling-est sweetest boy. The days were one long round of petting and coddling, of wild outpourings of affection. She could not do enough for him. She would bathe him over and over, change his clothes a dozen times a day.

The old man—not an old man, then, but much older than she was—had protested mildly. But he never actually interfered. He was very much in love with her, very happy in the status of family man. And it took no more than a few tears or a hurt look from either of them, woman or boy, to silence him immediately.

Only once, to Dusty's recollection, had his Dad (call him that; he had always called him that) demonstrated anything resembling firmness. That was when he, Dusty, was

about nine. He had insisted that the boy have his own
room and his own bed; he simply had to, he declared, and
that was that.

But that, as it turned out, was not that. Mr. Rhodes was
away from home a great deal during those days—lecturing
in winter, attending college for doctorate credit in summer.
And during these absences, his edict was generally
ignored.

They would start off to obey, go through all the prelimi-
naries. She would see him to his room, turn on the
nightlamp, tuck him under the bedclothes. She would tuck
him in very firmly, moving the bedclothes this way and
that, adjusting and readjusting the lamp. She would look
down at him, primly, her voice faltering a little as she
explained why things had to be as they were. "You understand, don't you, darling? Dad's so awfully good to us and
he knows what's best, and if he asks us to do something
even if it doesn't make any sense—well, we simply must!
It's not because Mother doesn't love you any more. She
l-loves her boy s-s-so much that . . . Oh, darling,
darling!"—a wail. "I can't! I *won't*. N-not tonight. Tomorrow but not tonight . . . "

He liked their bed best. It was larger than his, of course,
and he derived a strangely satisfying sense of security from
being in it. He did not always feel secure, otherwise,
despite the daily demonstrations of her and his father's
love. Almost always there was a feeling of unsatisfied
want, of something withheld. Of incompleteness. But there
with her in the big bed, just the two of them alone, he at
last knew absolute safety: the haunting, indefinable hunger
was fed. And he wanted for nothing.

He believed he had been about eleven when it happened.
It was on a Sunday morning, and she had been awakened
early by a rainstorm, and so she had awakened him (not
intentionally) with drowsy kisses and hugs. He burrowed
close to her. He moved his head, sleepily, feeling an unusual softness and warmth. And suddenly he felt it withdrawn, or, rather, since he did not release his hold, an
attempt at withdrawal.

"Bill! Let go, darling!"

"Huh?" He opened his eyes, unwillingly. "What's the

matter?"

"Well, you can see, can't you?"—her voice was almost sharp. "I mean, Mother has to fix her nightgown."

She fixed it hastily, blushing. She lay back down, rather stiffly, and then, seeing the innocence of his expression, she drew him close again.

"I'm sorry, darling. Mother didn't mean to sound cross to her baby."

"I'm not your baby," he said, and this time it was he who drew away from her.

"You're—? Oh, well, of course, you're not. Now you're Mother's big boy, her little man."

"I never was your baby," he said.

"B-but, sweetheart"—she raised up on one elbow, looked down troubledly into his face. "Of course, you were my baby. You still are. Has someone—did someone tell you that—"

"I know," he said. "I know what those are for. They're for babies, what Mamas feed babies with, and you never did so I'm not."

"But"—she laughed uncomfortably. A faint crimson was tinging the pale gold of her face, spreading down over her neck and into the deep shadowed hollow of her breasts. "But, sweetheart"—there was a catch to her laugh. "Of course, I did. You just don't remember!"

"No," he said, "I wasn't your baby, so you wouldn't want me to."

"But I would! I mean, I did! When you were a baby, I always—well, I always did!"

He turned his body, turning his back to her. She tried to put her arms around him, and he jerked away roughly.

"Darling! It's true, darling. You don't think Mother would lie, do you?"

He didn't answer her.

"You've g-got to believe me, dearest. You were always my baby, no one's but mine. Why whose baby would you be if . . . if . . . "

He didn't answer her.

"Now listen to me, Bill! I will not let you carry on like this! It's an extremely foolish way for you to act, and . . . Oh, darling! My poor darling! What can I say to you?"

Silence.

"Darling . . . honey lamb . . . Mother wasn't angry a moment ago. She didn't really mind. She wouldn't have minded a bit if you were still a little baby l-like . . . You understand, don't you, darling?"

Silence.

"If I . . . Would it be all right, darling, would you believe me if I—we—If now . . . ?"

He was still silent, but it was a different kind of silence. Warm, expectant, deliciously shivery. They lay very still for a moment, and then she sat up, and there was the sound of soft silk against silken flesh.

She lay back down. She whispered, "B-baby. Turn around, baby . . ." And he turned around.

Then, right on the doorstep of the ultimate heaven, the gates clanged shut.

She lay perfectly still, breathing evenly. She did not need to push him away, not physically. Her eyes did that. Delicately flushed a moment before, the lovely planes of her face were now an icy white.

"You're a very smart boy, Bill."

"Am I, Mother?"

"Very. Far ahead of your years. How long have you been planning this?"

"P-planning what, Mother?"

"You had it all figured out, didn't you? Your—poor old Dad, sick and worn out so much of the time. And me, still young and foolish and giddy, and loving you so much that I'd do anything to save you hurt."

"I-you mad at me about somethin', Mother?"

"Stop it! Stop pretending! Don't deceive yourself, Bill. At least be honest with yourself."

"M-Mother. I'm sorry if I—"

"Not nearly as sorry as I am, Bill. Nor as shocked, or frightened . . ."

She was frightened. And being unable to live with her fear, she tried to deny its existence. It had never happened, she told herself—and she told him. That rainy Sunday morning was a bad dream, or at worst no more than a misunderstanding, exaggerated out of true and innocent proportion by sleep-drugged minds. It had no reality, she said, and should be forgotten completely. And he did forget—almost. His conscious memory forgot.

He was her son. He understood the importance of believing that, and so he believed. And ostensibly—even in the eyes of Mr. Rhodes—there was no change in their relationship. No untoward change. She was still lovingly affectionate with the boy, absorbed in his welfare. He was still mutely adoring in her presence. True, there was no longer any pouting and arguing about Bill's sleeping arrangements. And, true, the caresses exchanged between woman and boy seemed considerably less fervent. But that, those things, were as they should be. Bill was growing up. Naturally he was pulling away from his mother's apron strings.

Dusty rolled restlessly on the bed, still thinking. His disinterest in girls, his "lack of time" for them: was she the reason? She was. He admitted it now. She had been the woman, the only one. Until he met her counterpart, in Marcia Hillis, there could be no other.

So the years passed, and everything *was* forgotten. As far as it is within human capacity to forget. Mr. Rhodes remained active, but his health was failing. Their concern for him, and the necessity to take care of him, drew the two well members of the family closer and closer together.

There were long, almost nightly discussions in the living room after the old man had retired. Conferences held in whispers, lights dimmed, so as not to disturb him. There were cups of coffee shared, and cigarettes passed back and forth. There was an intimacy of silences and sighs. Occasionally there were tears, with Dusty soothing her, drawing her head against his shoulder and stroking the thick lustrous gray hair.

All the awkwardness between them disappeared. The bond of trust and interdependence strengthened. Some nights she fell asleep, and he carried her up to her room . . . a room no longer shared with her husband.

The first night it happened, she had waked up. She kept her eyes closed but he knew she was awake, and for a terrible moment he was afraid she might scream or strike out at him. Still, since there was nothing to do but go ahead he went ahead, slipping off her robe, laying the thin-gowned body between the covers and carefully tucking them around its curving richness. Then, very gently, he had given her a chaste kiss on the forehead. And started to tip-toe from the room.

So I knew what I was doing. What of it? Was I supposed to make myself look like a heel?

She whispered, "Bill . . . " and he went back. She stretched out her arms, and he went down on his knees at her bedside, and the arms locked around him. "Bill, my darling Bill . . . " Her lips moved over his face. "How could I ever have—what would I ever do without you? You've been so good, so wonderful!"

"You're pretty wonderful yourself," he said. "And now you're going to sleep. Right now, young lady, under-stand?"

With superhuman effort, he forced himself to disengage her arms, to stand up and walk out of the room. It left him unnerved, sleepless throughout the night, but it proved worthwhile. The last shred of her caution was struck away. Carrying her to her room became an almost nightly hap-pening, even when she did not fall asleep. She would demand it, playfully, moving drowsily into his embrace. "S-oo tired, Bill. Help the old sleepy-head upstairs, hmm . . . ?"

Her weariness was not pretended, he knew. She had worried herself into exhaustion, and the long years of sex-ual starvation, or near-starvation, had robbed her of vital-ity. Now, at last, she had someone to lean upon, someone who loved as unselfishly as she. So she leaned willingly, anxiously.

The Free Speech petition . . . well, the old man had reacted exactly as he thought he would about that. He wasn't sure that he hadn't signed. In any event, he would not deny that he had and thus indirectly damn a cause he had believed in. He had stood pat, and, of course, the school board had promptly booted him out of his job. And with his failing health, the blow was almost fatal.

But, no. NO—Dusty almost shouted the word. That wasn't the way it was. It had worked out that way, but he hadn't planned it. A street-corner solicitor had offered him the petition, and he had signed it . . . without even thinking of the consequences. He had signed it simply William Bryant Rhodes, because there had not been enough space to add the Jr. (That was the only reason.) And he definitely had not faked his father's signature. Dad had taught him how to write. It was only natural that their signatures should be very similar.

She had been almost hysterical that night. She had been denied so much, real motherhood, real wifehood; she had had so little, and now that little—the modest security—had been lost. She was frightened; she was bewildered. In the dimly lit living-room, she lay sobbing in Dusty's arms, weeping and clinging to him like a lost child. Slowly drawing strength from his strength, reassurance from his softly whispered words.

She sniffled, and began to smile. He held a handkerchief to her nose and she blew obediently.

"J-just look at me," she smiled tremulously. "What a big cry-baby!"

"My baby," he said. "My little baby. And you just cry all you want to."

"Oh, B-Bill! Darling! W-what would I ever do without—"

"Nothing. Because I'll always be with you. Now. Hold still a minute and . . . "

He took the handkerchief and tapped the tears from her face. Very business-like, he tapped them from her neck . . . From her half-exposed breasts.

"My," he said, "a little bit more and you'd have been soaking." And he cupped one of his hands over the bare flesh. "You just ought to feel yourself."

He looked up, then, forced himself to, and he saw the shadows in her eyes. Then, his eyes narrowed, lazily, and she buried her face against his chest. And she whispered, "You shouldn't do that, Bill. You know you shouldn't. Never ever."

"Why not?" he said. "If you knew how much I loved you . . ."

"I know. I love you, too, darling. You've been so wonderful, so good to me that—Oh, Bill, sweet"—she tightened her arms desperately—"I wish I could tell you how much you mean to me."

Her body stiffened and went limp. He withdrew his hand, shifted her gently from his lap to the lounge. She lay there, motionless, hardly seeming to breathe, one arm flung across her face.

He hesitated. Then, kneeling, he turned back her robe, and pulled up her nightgown, and . . .

Her open palm exploded against his face.

It rocked him back on his heels, and he sat down on the floor. She sat up, readjusting her nightclothes.

"I had to be sure," she said, quietly. "I couldn't believe that you meant what you seemed to—I hated to believe it. But I had to be sure . . . "

. . . Then, she had begun to scream at him . . . bastard . . . filth . . . monster . . . pouring out her hatred and disgust.

Fortunately, Mr. Rhodes had taken a heavy sedative before retiring.

. . . The fan hummed drowsily. Stretched out before its warm, narcotic breeze, Dusty relived that terrible scene with his foster mother and found it not so terrible after all. He was glad that he had done this, forced himself to honestly re-examine the past. Taken bit by bit, looked at in the light of background happenings, he had only reacted normally to an abnormal situation. It was her fault, not his. She had been the aggressor, not he. Probably, if he had been a little more adroit, a little less clumsy, she would have done what he wanted her to. And what she undoubtedly wanted him to do to her.

No, it wasn't so bad, and he wasn't so bad. On the whole, he had behaved, and was behaving, a lot more decently than most guys.

He didn't hate Dad. He got a little annoyed with him, depressed when he thought of being saddled with him for years to come—but who wouldn't? He didn't hate him, certainly, and most certainly he didn't wish him dead.

And Bascom. He didn't hate Bascom, nor wish him dead . . . even if it was possible to bring his death about. Bascom had rubbed his nose into the dirt for months. Now, the old guy was scared out of his wits, and it was his, Dusty's, turn to do some rubbing. And why should he have been disturbed about doing it?

Tug Trowbridge. He felt no admiration for Tug, no identification with him. It had been up to Tug to rescue him from a trap. Naturally, since the matter was vital to him, he had been keenly interested in its success. That was all there was to it.

Marcia Hillis . . .

Well, his attitude toward her was harder to analyze. First, he had been sick with concern for her. Then, the concern had shifted to something that was almost hate. She had been the prey, and they the hunters, and when it seemed that she might escape—as he had hoped she would a moment before—he had almost hated her.

Well. But was that so odd, after all? He had much the same mixed feelings about that other *her*, his foster mother. And there had been a parallel situation in that case. He had been afraid that she might tell Dad—dreadfully, sickeningly afraid. So loving her, unable to keep from loving her, he had also hated her. He had wanted her punished for the terror she had caused him.

Now, well, now, of course, he only loved her; he would have loved her if she had still been alive. And now that the danger to himself was past, he felt only love—he could think of no other way to describe his feelings—for Marcia Hillis. He would talk to Tug tonight. Find out where she had gone. Then, when Dad died . . . if he died . . . or sometime, somehow, he would get in touch with her. Go to her or have her come back here. She liked him. He was sure of that, despite this thing she had tried to do for financial gain. So . . . so they would be together, and this time it would be different The scene would be the same but this time . . .

. . . *no sudden, terrifying blow in the face. No icy voice, no hatefully screamed reproaches. Only the yielding ivory body, the warm welcoming arms, the mass of hair tumbling silkily over his face . . . And, at last, fulfillment.*

Dusty stirred restlessly. His eyes dragged open, and after a minute's more tossing, he sat up. He lighted a cigarette, blew the smoke out in nervous, excited puffs.

It would be like that. It *had* to be, he realized now. Through the years, he had been so formed that he could accept only one woman. And without her there could be nothing — no rest, no peace, no completion. Only an aching void where strange fears dwelled and multiplied, and gnawed unceasingly.

He had to have her, and he would. She liked him. He

made good money—and there were ways of making more—and if she'd been desperate enough to attempt . . .

Dimly, he heard the phone ring. Then, his father's voice answering it, and his footsteps shuffling back from the living room. He stood up, just as the old man opened the door.

"Hate to call you, Bill, but someone from the hotel . . . "

Dusty muttered a curse. "You've already told them I was here? Well, okay."

He thrust his way past Mr. Rhodes, and snatched up the phone. Then, forcing his voice to a semblance of politeness, he said, "Yes, sir. This is Bill Rhodes."

"How are you, fellow?"—it was Tug Trowbridge. "Sorry to wake you up, but I figured you and me had better have a little talk . . . Now, yeah."

Ten miles out of the city, the broad new highway was paralleled for perhaps a mile by an abandoned strip of blacktop pavement. It lay on the other side of the railroad tracks, gradually curving off through the hills and becoming lost in a wasteland of deserted farms. It was there, just over the crest of the first hill, that Dusty met Tug Trowbridge.

He parked his coupe behind the gangster's big black Cadillac. Tug beamed and extended a bottle of beer as Dusty slid into the seat next to him.

"Ain't this a scorcher, kid? Here, get a load of this inside of you and you'll feel better"

Dusty jerked his head nervously. "I don't drink, thanks. W-what did you—"

"Not even beer? Well"—Tug elevated the bottle and swallowed, gurglingly—"you could do a lot worse, kid. A guy's got to let off a little steam some way, and beer's about the safest thing I know of."

He belched, and tossed the bottle through the window. Reaching over the seat, he reached another bottle from a pail of ice. He pulled the cap with his teeth, took a long, thoughtful drink. He stared through the windshield absently, belching again.

"Yes, sir," he said. "A man can do a lot worse than drink beer."

"About last night," said Dusty. "Was that what—"

"Yeah," Tug said. "Last night, now there's an example. You stick to beer after this, fellow, and leave the babes alone. It'll save you a lot of trouble. Save everyone a lot of trouble."

Dusty's face flushed. "But it wasn't like that! It was like I told you! She called for some stationery, and then when I went in she—"

"So who cares," Tug shrugged, indifferently, "but that wasn't her story. And, kid, she seemed plenty legit to me. She talked it and she had the stuff to back it up. Newspaper clippings and letters and so on. It looked like she was just what she claimed to be—a high-class nightclub dancer. Came to town early figuring she might pick up an engagement during the races."

"But that doesn't mean—"

"Sure, I know. Maybe she'd just started on the make. Or maybe she just used the legit as a cover-up for the other. Maybe. But that little maybe could cause a hell of a lot of trouble. You put that maybe in there, and it's an entirely different deal from the one I figured on. Give some shakedown baby the heave-ho, that's nothing. She can't squawk or if she does squawk it don't do her no good. But a woman like this one—someone who can prove she's legitimate, or maybe make it impossible for you to prove that she ain't—well . . . "

He raised the bottle to his lips. Covertly, out of the corners of his shrewd animal's eyes, he studied Dusty's pale face. He grinned to himself, forcing his features into a thoughtful scowl.

"Not nice, huh, kid? I saw we'd caught a hot one right away, but of course it was too late to let go then. We had to go ahead, me and three of my boys, and I'm telling you, they don't like it much either. They got their necks stuck out to here—they have and you have and I have. And that little lady says just a few words, and all five are going to pop."

"P-pop?"

"Pop," Tug nodded solemnly. "Attempted rape. Kidnaping. They ain't the same thing as running through a traffic signal, kid, or spitting on the sidewalk. They particularly ain't the same thing down here in the south."

"But it's just her word—"

"Huh-uh. Not that her word wouldn't be plenty against us, a bellboy and three heavies, but there's a lot more than that. Think it over, Dusty. Probably a dozen people saw that little frammis this morning. It didn't mean anything to them at the time, but they saw it. And they'll talk just as soon as she does."

Think it over? Dusty's eyes were glazing. God, he didn't need to think it over. "Isn't there some way t-to to—?"

"Yes," said Tug, slowly. "There's a way. I'd sure hate to do it, and the boys don't like it either, but . . . "

His voice trailed off into silence. Dusty stared at him, not immediately understanding, and then his face went a shade paler.

"No!" he gasped. "No! You can't do that!"

"We-el"—Tug gave him another covert glance. "Like I say, I'd sure hate to. With some babes, it would almost be a pleasure, but a dame like her—real class and all kinds of looks and a shape that's out of this world, why . . . "

"You w-won't do it, will you? Promise you won't!"

"We-el . . . You know where you can lay your hands on ten thousand dollars?"

"Ten thous— Of course not!"

"Neither do I. But that's what it's got to be, Dusty. That or the other. For ten grand she keeps quiet. She puts it down in black and white that none of us laid a finger on her, and she left the hotel of her own free will."

He paused, again studying the bellboy, smiling again secretly. He went on, frowning earnestly. "When I say I ain't got it, I mean it, kid. It's strictly under your hat, see, but I'm broke. I'm a hell of a lot worse than broke."

"But"—Dusty shook his head, incredulously—"but how—"

"I can still flash a roll? Drive a big car? Pay heavy rent? Yeah, I can do it—for a couple more weeks. I've been slipping for a long time, Dusty, and now I'm right down at the bottom of the sack. I'm broke. I've got a hell of a big income-tax rap hanging over me. I've been stalling it for years, and now I can't stall any longer. I either pay up or else." He sighed, flung the emptied bottle out the window. "Of course, it makes it easy for me in a way. The spot I'm in, this dame could yell her head off and she couldn't make it much worse."

"B-but—"

"Sure," Tug nodded. "There's you and the boys to think about. And of course I don't like to just sit still and wait for old Uncle Whiskers to sock it to me. If I can't do anything better, I'd like to get a big enough roll to skip the country."

He lapsed into another silence, his big good-natured face long with concern. His big face that looked good-natured turned toward the window. There was a small mirror there, attached to the windscreen. It gave him a full view of Dusty's tortured features.

He sighed heavily, shifted the sound into an absently amused laugh. "Y'know it's a funny thing, kid—about this Hillis woman, I mean. You might think she'd be sore as hell at you, but she don't seem to be at all. In fact, I kind of got the idea that she liked you a lot. She's been pushed around and she figures she ought to be paid for it. But there's nothing personal in it, see? Why, I'll bet if you were in the chips—you'd have to be, of course, with a babe like that—I'll bet she'd come a running to you like—"

"I've got to know," said Dusty. "I've got to know the truth, Mr. Trowbridge. Is she—"

"Yeah? And why don't you just make it Tug, kid?"

"I've got to know, Tug. Is she—you haven't already killed her?"

"Huh!" Tug exclaimed. "Why, of course, we ain't, and we ain't going to if there's another way out. We got her hid nice and comfortable, a lot more comfortable than you and me are right now."

"Could I—could I see her?"

"Sure you can," Tug said evenly. "If you think I'm lying, just say so and I'll take you to her."

Dusty hesitated. Then, the implications of Tug's statement hit him full force, and he shook his head firmly. He had to believe the gangster. At least, he couldn't appear to doubt him. For if Tug had ordered her death to keep her quiet, and if he was forced to admit the fact . . . well, he,

Dusty, would also be quieted. Similarly. Permanently.

Tug would feel compelled to do it, and not merely to protect himself. The big man was desperate. He wanted something from Dusty and he intended to get it, and the woman was vital to his getting—a means of enforcing his demands. She had to be alive, then. He could not openly doubt that she was alive. To do so would be to make himself useless to Tug—a man with dangerous knowledge who refused to cooperate—and he would not live long.

Dusty thought it was that way, but he wasn't positive. He spoke cautiously, testing his theory:

"There's one thing I don't understand, Tug. You figure on jumping the country, anyway? Well, then, why not just let this woman go when you're ready to jump? Let her talk all she wants to. You won't be around to face the music."

"Well"—Tug shifted in the seat—"I, uh, couldn't hardly do that, kid. An income-tax rap is one thing. Kidnaping and abetting a rape is somethin' else."

"But you wouldn't be around. You don't intend to come back."

"Well, uh, like I said a moment ago, there's you and the boys to think about. We're all in this together, and you'd still be here, and—" He broke off, eyes glinting. "I say something funny, kid?"

"No"—Dusty shook his head. "I just wanted to know how things stood."

"Okay!" Tug snapped harshly. "Now you know. Now you got the picture. I got some plans and I ain't letting 'em be screwed up. I didn't figure you in 'em originally, but that's the way it's worked out. You're in and you're going to play. Or else!"

Furiously, he reached over the seat and snatched up another bottle of beer. The cap grated against his teeth, popped loose, and he spat it out and drank.

He coughed, leaning back in the seat, and the old joviality came back into his voice. A little strained, but nonetheless there.

"Aaahh, kid. This is no way for pals to talk to each other, and I've always been your pal, ain't I? Always friendly and easy to get along with, and tossing the dough around. I liked you, see? I felt like you were my kind of people and I know you felt the same way about me. Why, who did you come to this morning when you were in a real jam? Why, you came to me, didn't you, and I didn't hesitate a minute, did I? I had plenty big worries of my own, but I just said, Why, sure, Dusty. Just leave it to me and I'll take care of it. Ain't that right, now?"

"That's right," Dusty murmured.

"And I didn't know what I was getting into, didn't I? I didn't have the slightest idea that it was going to work out so's I could put the squeeze—ask you to do me a favor. Help me out and put yourself on easy street at the same time. I didn't have any idea it was going to be that way. All I knew was—that you were a pal, and I was ready to knock myself out to give you a hand . . . "

His voice droned on earnestly . . . pals . . . favors . . . give you a hand . . . didn't know. And Dusty nodded earnestly. Fighting to keep his sudden excitement from showing in his face.

Suppose Tug *had* known. Suppose he had arranged the whole thing! It made sense, didn't it? It made sense to a degree that no other explanation could approach. It explained things that could be explained in no other way.

Bascom. Why had he allowed Marcia Hillis to register—a woman alone, arriving late at night? Why, because Tug had told him to and he had been afraid to refuse. And the ten-dollar room? Why, the answer to that was beautifully simply, too. There were only a few such rooms in the hotel, and one of them was on Tug's floor. Without arousing Dusty's suspicions, she had been put right where Tug wanted her—and wanted him—when she sprang the trap. The circumstance would practically impel his appeal to the gangster. His old pal, Tug, would be right there at hand, and he would run to him automatically.

The kidnaping. The "kidnaping." And he had been afraid that they wouldn't get away with it—justifiably afraid. For they wouldn't have got away with the real thing. They wouldn't even have attempted the real thing. It was all an act, part of the scheme to make him vulnerable to Tug's demands.

There were a few loose ends to the theory, but on the whole it made a very neat package. And relatively, at least, it was as comfortable as it was plausible. If Marcia Hillis was working with Tug, then naturally she was in no danger. If she worked with Tug, then she was attainable by him, Dusty. Not through money alone, of course. Despite the part she had played, or appeared to have played, he didn't believe that she could be influenced very far or very long by money alone. But certainly, with a woman like that, money would be an essential. She would expect it, take it for granted. And with Tug's help, by helping Tug with his scheme, whatever that scheme was . . .

"Just a minute, kid." Tug leaned over him, flipped open the door of the glove compartment. "I know you maybe think I'm giving you a snow job about that babe, so take a gander at this."

He drew it out of the compartment, a crumpled eight-by-ten oblong of glossy cardboard. He smoothed it out carelessly and handed it to the bellboy, and Dusty's breath sucked in with a gasp. It was her picture, a theatrical shot, with her name written along the bottom in white ink. She was posed against a background of artificial palms; she lay, smiling, along the sloping trunk of one. A wisp of some thinly leafed vine was between her thighs. Her hands, fingers spread in a revealing lattace, lay over her breasts. Otherwise she was nude.

"Well, kid"—Tug took the picture from his hands and crammed it back into the compartment—"she's just what I said, huh? I wasn't lying, was I?"

Dusty shook his head. So she was an entertainer, or had been one. That still didn't prove that she wasn't working with Tug.

"A lot of woman, huh, Dusty?" Tug smacked his lips. "You ever see anything like her in your life?"

"No. I mean not quite, I guess," Dusty said.

"But she ain't got a bit more on the ball than you, Dusty. For a man, you've got just as much as she has. All the looks and the class that she has, and then some."

"And you really think"—Dusty cleared his throat—"you really think that she would—that she might—"

"That she'd go for you? If you were in the chips? I'll tell you what I think, kid." Tug tapped him solemnly on the knee. "I'd guarantee it, know what I mean? Yes, sir, I'd guarantee she would."

Dusty hesitated. It was all wrong. He was all mixed up. Tug had aroused first one instinct, then another; played upon one after another. Self-preservation, avarice, fear for her, outright desire. He had offered too much, too eagerly; threatened too much. And the end result was confusion, or, more accurately, the canceling out of everything he had said.

She was in no danger, Dusty guessed. He guessed that he was in none—none that he could not escape from with a little fast thinking. At this point, he could still pull out with no harm to anyone but Tug. And, yet . . .

Well, he was only guessing, wasn't he? He might be figuring the thing wrong, and if he was she'd be lost to him. Dead. And if he was right, she would still be lost to him. He would have to go on as he was now, barely getting by from one day to the next. Trudging through a gray emptiness that grew emptier and grayer with every step.

He shivered innwardly; he couldn't stand it, even the thought of it. But could he—could he, on the other hand, accept the sinister alternative? Could he adopt a course which must certainly run counter to all the plans and preparations of years?

His voice faltered. "I don't know, Tug. It seems kind of crazy that I should even be thinking about . . . well, what we've been talking about. You see, I've always wanted to be a doctor, my father and mother wanted me to be one. I was just working at the hotel— temporarily until—"

"Yeah?" Tug chuckled softly. "Who you trying to kid, kid? You're there at the hotel because the easy money's there, and you're an easy money guy. I know, see? I can spot 'em a mile off. Maybe you think different, but I know. You wouldn't go back to school if you was paid to."

"But I—"

"We've talked enough, Dusty. A lot longer than I figured on talking to you. But maybe I ought to tell you one thing more. Them boys of mine are pretty jumpy. They're pretty leery of you, kid. If they got the notion that you might jump the wrong way, I don't know as I could hold 'em in line."

Tug nodded at him grimly, and abruptly the doubts and confusion were dispelled from Dusty's mind. He didn't know Tug's hoods, as he knew Tug. He had never been friendly with them. To them he would just be a stumbling block, a guy who'd made trouble and might make more. And what they might do, *would* do, was reasonably easy to predict.

". . . . won't be around much longer, y'know, kid. They'll be on their own. So what's it going to be?"

What was it going to be? What could it be? The choice was not his.

"All right," he said. "All right, Tug. What do you want me to do?"

And Tug told him.

As the body has its limits to suffer, so is the mind limited to shock. One can be startled just so much, alarmed just so much, and then there can be no more. The wheel of emotions becomes stalled on dead-center. And instead of turmoil there is calm.

So with Dusty. In little more than an hour a whole way of life had been jerked from beneath him and a new one proffered. He had been pushed to the outermost boundaries of shock; now he answered Tug quietly:

"It can't be done, Tug. Those deposit boxes are theft proof. It takes two keys for each one, the hotel's and the depositor's, and even if you could get them both . . . "

"Yeah? Go on, kid."

"There's a box for each room. It would take all night to unlock them all. And you wouldn't know whether they were worth robbing unless you did open them. I couldn't tell you. Practically all the deposits are made in the day time and—"

"Uh-huh, sure," Tug interrupted. "I know all that. Maybe I'd better lay it on the line for you, huh?"

"Maybe you'd better."

"The racing season starts the week after next. All the big bookies will drift in next week. They'll want to look over the track, study the early workouts, and so on. They'll be loaded with cash. There's no damned guess work about it, see? They'll have the dough, and with the hours they keep, they'll have to bank with the hotel. So we make 'em for their keys, say, six or seven of the biggest operators, and we hit the jackpot. We knock down a couple hundred grand, maybe a quarter of a million, in five minutes."

"Yes, but . . . " Dusty licked his lips. "How do you mean, make 'em for their keys? You mean you'd—you'd—"

"Naah." Tug nudged him jovially. "Nothing like it, kid. I'll just throw a little party for 'em up in my suite; hell, they've been to plenty of my parties in the past. Then, me and the boys will give 'em a little surprise. Knock them out and hogtie them, y'know. Take 'em out of circulation for a while."

"Well . . . " Dusty hesitated. "But that still leaves the hotel keys. Bascom"—he paused again. "God, I can't do that, Tug! Bascom will be right there; and there's no way I could use the keys without—"

"Hold it. Hold it!" said Tug. "You ain't going to use them. Bascom is. All you're going to do is take the dough and lock it up in the checkroom. Put it in a satchel I'll give you and check it, just like it was a regular piece of baggage. I—"

"But Bascom! What about him?"

"—don't want it with me, see, in case of a foul-up. My boys might get a little excited, know what I mean? They might get to quarreling over the split. So you check it and tear up the stub—memorize the number first, of course—and I'll get in touch with you as soon as the heat dies down."

"Yes, but—"

"I'll split the take with you, kid. A full half for you and the other for me and the boys. You hang on to yours a few months, and then you get yourself fired, and—"

"I asked you about Bascom!" Dusty insisted. "Now, what about him?"

Tug's eyes shifted for a moment. He looked out into the brilliant sunlight, gaze narrowed musingly, and then he again looked at Dusty.

"All right, kid. I guess I'd better spread it all out. But you don't know from nothing, see? You don't know nothing about Bascom. He don't know that you and me got a deal."

"I understand."

"One of my connections tipped me off to Bascom three-four months ago. He's on the lam from a pen back east, crashed out with twenty years to serve of a thirty-year bank-robber rap. One word from me, and he'll be back doing time again."

"Well . . . oh," said Dusty, and he nodded, remembering.

"They asked you about it, huh?" Tug grinned out of the corner of his mouth. "You know why I wrote that letter to the management, kid? Because of the way he was treating you. Yeah, I noticed it all right—I notice plenty. You did everything you could to get along with him, and all he could do was make it tough for you. I spoke to him, and he covered up while I was around. But I knew he hadn't stopped. So I figured I'd better give him a real jolt."

"Well," Dusty said, "that was, uh, certainly nice of you. But I still—"

"I know. I know just what you're going to say. You're going to say that Bascom can't play ball on this deal. If he does, he'll do his twenty years and maybe twenty more on top of it. But here's the angle, see? He plays, but it don't look like he does. He has a gun drawn on him and he loses his nerve, acts like a goddamned dope instead of—"

"He'll never get away with it." Dusty shook his head. "He just *can't*, Tug! A man on the outside of the cashier's cage couldn't cover a man on the inside with a gun. The window opening is too small. The cashier, the man on the inside, could just drop down to the floor or move a little to one side and he'd be out of range."

"He could if he thought fast enough. If he wasn't scared out of his pants."

"You can't make it look good," Dusty said doggedly. "They're bound to know that it was an inside job."

"Huh-uh. Maybe they think it is but they can't prove it. All they can prove is that Bascom ain't much of a hero, that he didn't use good judgment."

"I can't see it," Dusty frowned. "They'll never—I mean, I don't think they'll ever believe he was held up. Not from the outside. Now if there was a guy on the inside—one of the lobby porters, say—it would be different. He could be working in there and suddenly stick a gun in Bascom's ribs, and Bascom would have to come across. He couldn't get away, and—and—"

He swallowed, leaving the sentence unfinished. There was a long moment of silence, with Tug staring at him steadily, and then he found his voice again.

"Bascom. He's willing a take that kind of chance?"

"It's a chance," Tug shrugged. "If he don't take it, he doesn't have any chance at all. I see that he goes back to the pen."

"Well . . . " Dusty said. "And what about me? Where am I supposed to be while all this is going on?"

"Right there in the cashier's cage with him. Helping him with the work like you always are around two-thirty in the morning. You've got to be there, see? That money satchel will be too big to squeeze through the window, and there won't be time to chase all the way around the counter. You'll have to grab it and get rid of it fast."

"But that leaves me on the spot, too! If I'm right there—"

"How does it? You're just a bellboy; Bascom's your boss. You're supposed to try to stop him, risk getting yourself killed, if he's willing to open the boxes? Huh-uh, they couldn't expect it of you, kid. They'd think you was a damned fool if you tried it."

"Well," Dusty nodded, "maybe. I suppose you're right about that. But—well, what about the other? When I take the satchel and check it? You said that Bascom wasn't supposed to know anything about me, that I was in on the deal. But—"

"He don't. He won't. And you don't know anything, get me? Nothing about him, and nothing about what's coming off."

"But if I take the money right in front of him—"

"Kid," Tug sighed. "Dusty, boy. Jesus Christ, ain't there any goddamned little thing you can leave to me? You think I just dreamed up this caper five minutes ago?"

"No. But—"

"Bascom won't see you! When he gets back up near the window I grab him by the tie and slug him. Knock him unconscious. He'll hold still for it, see; it helps to make the thing look good. I knock him out cold, and he'll still be out when you get back from checking the dough and lock yourself into the cage again. So far as anyone knows you never left the cage."

"But if the satchel won't go through the window opening, he's bound to—"

"Goddammit, I—! It goes through when it's empty, don't it? It's got to, don't it? So on the return trip, I maybe take out part of the dough. Stuff it into my pocket or down the front of my shirt."

Glaring, his face mottled with irritation, Tug snatched another bottle from the pail. He almost slammed the cap against his teeth, jerked it with a grunt of pain. And drank. He did not lower the bottle until it was emptied.

"Sorry, kid" —he forced an apologetic laugh. "I don't blame you for wanting to know the score, of course. But, Jesus, every damned little thing! It kind of sounds like you thought I was a boob. Like maybe you didn't trust me."

"No," Dusty said hastily. "No, I don't feel that way. Its just—well, mixed up. There's so many things that might go wrong, and if anything does—"

"Nothing will." Tug dropped a friendly hand to his shoulder. "Let me tell you something, Dusty. It always seems that way when a guy's going on a caper. Always, particularly if it's his first one. He gets to thinking that everyone knows what he knows, that they see all the little holes he sees and that they're liable to reach through and grab him. But it ain't that way, y'understand! He's the guy with the answers, the only guy. The others—they don't see nothing or know nothing, or if they do it don't mean nothing to 'em."

Dusty nodded reluctantly. He hadn't said what he wanted to, he hadn't got to the heart of his concern, and he couldn't know. A gate had closed in his mind, blocking the words, cutting off the half-formed thought that lay behind them.

"Look at it this way, kid . . . I'm not taking the dough with me, am I? You know I'm not just giving you a line about that?"

Yes— Dusty's lips moved wordlessly—he was quite sure of that. Positive of it.

"It'll be just like I said. You'll check the dough, and tear up the stub. You'll have to do it, see? The cops are going to talk to you, and they just accidentally might frisk you. Anyway, it just ain't a good thing to have around. There's too damned many things that could happen to it."

I know— Dusty's lips moved again. Memorize the number. Tear up the stub. Yes, that was the way it would have to be.

"Well, there you are, kid. There's only one way in the world I can get to that dough, get my share of it. And that's through you. So I can't let anything happen to you, can I? I've got to be sure that everything's going to go smooth, and that you'll come through without a rumble. I *got* to, see? I've got to be sure, and I am sure. Why, hell, I'd be crazy to pull the deal otherwise, now wouldn't I?"

Dusty nodded. He agreed with that, also. For his own sake, Tug would have to be positive of his safety. But, still . . .

He couldn't say it. That tiny gate in his mind had closed tightly, imprisoning, with similar shoddy and hideous prisoners, the thought that he could not yet consciously accept.

"That's it, Dusty. That's all of it. You play it absolutely safe, and you get a cool hundred grand for your share. At least a hundred grand. Hell"—Tug nudged him, grinning. "I'll even take care of the babe's ten g's out of my end."

"Well," Dusty murmured. "I . . . you, uh, don't need to do that. But, well, I was wondering about her, Tug. I mean, you said she was on the level, and—"

"So what? She's been around, she knows what the score is, she ain't some punk bobby-soxer with the mood in her eyes. Dames in her racket, kid—bouncing around in these nightclubs with everything showing but their appetite— they all belong to the same club. The let's-see-the-dough-honey-and-I'll-ask-you-no-questions."

Dusty laughed, a little unwillingly. Tug laughed with him, studying him, then continued, his voice confidentially low. "I'll tell you what, kid. If there ain't no hitch anywhere, like I'm sure there won't be, I'll put her in touch with you. Before we split the dough, yeah. We may have to wait quite a while for that, but there's no sense in you waiting for her. How'd you like that, huh? Connect with her right away, almost." He slapped the bellboy on the back, not waiting for an answer. "I'll fix it up for you, Dusty. You can count on it. Now about the dough, the split . . . "

"I was wondering about that," Dusty frowned. "You know, I can't carry any packages out of the hotel, Tug. I mean, they have to be opened and examined before they can be carried out. And—"

"Forget it," Tug interrupted. "I'll figure out something when the time comes."

"How will I — how will you get in touch with me?"

"I'll figure that out, too. It depends on how things are at the time, see? Just leave it to me, for Christ's sake—it's my headache, ain't it?—and stop knocking yourself out!"

His face had become flushed again, the irritation was back in his voice. Surlily, he hurled the emptied bottle through the window.

"Jesus, kid. I don't mean to blow my top at you, but—well, skip it. We're all set, right? We'll be running through it some more between now and next week, but we're all set. We've got an agreement."

"We're all set," Dusty said steadily— "We've got an agreement."

Strangely, during the time intervening between his meeting with Tug and the morning of the robbery, he felt quite calm, quite at peace with himself. Only when he tried to examine his feelings—studied their nominal strangeness—was there any rift in the peace. And even then his qualms were faint and of brief duration. There was simply nothing for them to feed upon.

His handsome, olive-skinned face was as unfurrowed, as openly honest, as ever. The wide-set eyes remained clear and unworried. His voice, his manner, the manifold minutiae which comprised personality—they were all normal. For, for the first time in his memory, all his self-doubts were gone and he felt sure of himself. He was about to be made whole. He knew it, and the inner knowledge was reflected in the outer man.

Despite Tug's ambiguity, the robbery would be successful. He knew it and it was all he needed to know. More important, most important, he would have Marcia Hillis. Despite Tug's intentions, good or bad, he would have her. He felt it, knew it, and *it* was all he needed to know.

In his new-found sureness, he was unusually patient with Mr. Rhodes. He was quietly pleasant and polite to Bascom—a Bascom who had become drawn-faced, shifty-eyed, moodily silent unless he was forced to speak. It was easy to be patient now, easy to be pleasant and polite. Feeling as he did—unconquerable and unfearful—he could not be any other way.

The sureness grew. It remained with him, strong and unwavering, during the most acid of tests—his meeting with I. Kossmeyer, attorney at law.

The second day after his fateful talk with Tug Trowbridge, the day bell captain handed Dusty a note when he came on duty. It was from Kossmeyer, a curt scrawl on one of the attorney's letterheads. It said, simply, *Rhodes: Think would be advisable for you to drop into my office tomorrow morning.*

Dusty shredded the note, and its enclosing envelope, into a wastebasket. He did not call at Kossmeyer's office. He didn't like the little attorney, and he had—he told himself—better things to do with his time.

Two mornings later, as he was leaving the hotel, Kossmeyer met him at the service entrance.

"Want to talk to you, Rhodes," he said, brusquely. "What about some coffee?"

"Certainly," Dusty nodded. "Wherever you say, Mr. Kossmeyer."

They took a booth in a nearby restaurant. Dusty sipped at his coffee, set it down and looked up. And for the first time in days he felt a ruffling of his calm.

Not that he was afraid. He certainly wasn't afraid of this little pipsqueak of a man. But he was extremely irritated, almost angered. He stared across the table, his irritation mounting, a red flush spreading over his face.

The attorney's eyes had become preternaturally wide, brimmed with an exaggerated sincerity that made mock of the term. He had tightened the skin of his face, smoothing away its habitual wrinkles, leaving it bland and untroubled. His lips were curled with serenity—a preposterous caricature of it—and his chin was slightly outthrust, posed at an angle of quiet defiance. He was dignity distorted, bravery become knavery, sanctimoniousness masking sin. He was a mirror, jeering at the subject it reflected. Yet so muted were the jeers, so delicate the inaccuracies of delineation, that they evaded detection. True and false were blended together. The false was merely an extended shadow of the true.

Dusty's flush deepened. Unconsciously, he tried to alter his expression, and the attorney's face moved, following the change. Now he was wounded ("wounded" with quotes). Now he was losing his temper—in the manner of a Grade-C movie hero. And now—then—he was himself again. Neither friendly nor unfriendly, simply a man doing a job in the best and quickest way possible.

"You see, Rhodes? It doesn't mean a goddamned thing, does it? It's what you've got inside that counts."

"What do you want with me?" Dusty snapped. "Say it and get it over with."

"I've already got part of it over, showed you that you're not kidding anyone but yourself. Anyway, you're sure as hell not kidding me. Now that you understand that, you can stop trying. Stop covering up and come clean. Why did you sign your father's name to that petition?"

"Why? Why would I—"

"That's right. Why would you, why did you?" The attorney leaned forward, his shrewd face suddenly sympathetic and understanding. "It was just one of those things, wasn't it, son? You signed it without thinking, without any idea of what the consequences might be. It never occurred to you that with you and your dad having the same name—with your signatures so much alike. . .I imagine he taught you how to write, didn't he? Probably set down examples for you when you were a kid, and had you try to copy 'em."

Dusty hesitated. He wanted to explain, to make someone else believe and thus bolster his own belief. The words were in his mouth, almost, practically ready to emerge.

"Sure," Kossmeyer continued, earnestly. "That's the way it was—couldn't have been any other way. Hell, a signature that good, it takes practice; you had to have had it right back from the beginning. And it was perfectly natural that you would have it. You were your dad's junior, an only child to boot. That always makes a kid something special. The father identifies with him more closely—sort of tries to form him into his own pattern. It's a protective gesture, I suppose. By making his son part of him, he. . . Excuse me. Yeah?"

"It was that way," Dusty nodded, slowly. "It—he— was even more that way with me, I imagine, than if I'd been his own son. Yes. . . that's right. I was adopted. It was so long ago that I can hardly remember it, and I doubt that Dad knows that I know. So—"

"Sure, I'd never mention it. He and the wife couldn't have any kids of their own?"

"I guess not. Probably she could have; she was a lot younger than he was, and I think she. . . well, that she was physically okay."

"Mmm. A very beautiful woman, wasn't she? I seem to have heard that she was."

"Yes."

"I've been wondering: have you any idea why she married a guy so much older?"

"They met while he was lecturing at college. She was trying to work her way through, and he helped her a lot, I guess, and she felt like she couldn't. . ."

Dusty caught himself, with a start. How had they gotten to talking about her? How, and why, had he been led so far from the original subject?

He said shortly, "What's all that got to do with it?"

"What?" The attorney's eyebrows shot up. "Why, nothing that I know of. Just being curious. A set-up like that always makes me kind of wonder. It's none of my business, of course, so don't take it the wrong way, but—"

"Yes?"

"I wonder if she didn't marry him because she loved him. Do you suppose that could have been it?"

"Well," Dusty nodded, hesitantly, "I suppose she did. Naturally."

"She just didn't give a damn about surface appearance, don't you imagine? She knew a right guy when she saw him, and she latched onto him."

He stared at Dusty, gravely: a man discussing an interesting but impersonal problem. His bright bird's eye moved thoughtfully over the other's face. And narrowed imperceptibly.

"Now, getting back to this signature deal. You didn't forge your dad's name. It just came natural to you, and you didn't have to forge it. That's about the case, isn't it?"

"Well"—Dusty examined the insidiously objectionable statement, and was unable to object to it—"well, yes."

"And you just kind of accidentally left off the junior part. Without thinking of the consequences. Your dad was a public figure; everyone was certain to associate that signature with him. But that never occurred to you. . .did it?"

"No, it didn't!" Dusty snapped. "I—look, I didn't even know what the petition was about. A woman on a street corner asked me to sign, so I signed. Like a lot of people did probably, just to be obliging."

"But you must have looked at it?"

"Certainly, I looked at it, but it didn't mean anything to me. You know how they phrase some of those things. You have to study them carefully to get at the meaning."

"Yeah," Kossmeyer nodded. "They get pretty cute sometimes. How was this one phrased?"

"Committee to Defend the Constitution—that was the heading. Then it said, 'Recognizing the vital importance of an unhampered exchange of ideas, I, the undersigned, hereby—"

His voice died on a strangled note.

Kossmeyer grinned at him wolfishly. "So you didn't know what it was all about, huh? It didn't mean a thing to you."

"I—no! No, it didn't. I read it afterwards, after the paper came out with the story."

"Yeah? And what about that junior deal? Why didn't you tack it onto your name?"

"Because there wasn't room for it! If I'd known how important it was going to be, of course, I'd have—"

"You had room for all the rest. First name, middle name, last—the whole damned handle, all written out big and bold so that even a blind man couldn't miss it. . .Don't try to horse-shit me, buster. You ain't even half-way smart enough."

"But you don't understand. . ." And he wanted him to. He wasn't afraid of Kossmeyer, but he did want him to understand. "I know it probably doesn't make much sense, but—"

"It makes plenty of sense." The attorney leaned forward grimly. "You've lived in this town all your life—you know how people think here, how they'd react to a thing like this Free Speech business. You grew up in a school-teacher's family, and you know what a teacher's problems are. How they can't even look crosseyed without some know-nothing bastard taking a pot-shot at 'em. You knew all that and you knew something else. You knew the old man was sick and that a blow like this one could easily kill him. And that's what you wanted, wasn't it? *You wanted him dead!*"

Dusty's mouth opened. It snapped shut again, and, quite calmly, he lighted a cigarette. He exhaled the smoke, staring back at Kossmeyer insolently.

"That's ridiculous. But as long as you seem to be so sure. . ."

"You know why. For the same reason I didn't come out to the house to see you. He's a swell guy, the kind this country needs a hell of a lot more of, and I didn't want to make things any harder for him. If he knew what kind of pure-d, rotten son-of-a-bitch he'd given his name to—"

"That's about enough," Dusty snapped. "I'm leaving."

"You'd better not," Kossmeyer assured him. "You do and you'll be the sorriest son-of-a-bitch in sixteen states."

"What"—Dusty sank back down into the booth—"what do you mean?"

"I can't do anything about what's happened. All I can do is kind of let the case die quietly. But that's for the past, the present. The future, that's something else, buster. You won't be so lucky next time. You pull another stunt on him, and, by God, I'll stick you for it. If there isn't a law I can do it under, I'll get one passed!"

"You're crazy," Dusty said, coldly. "This whole thing's crazy. Why would I do anything to hurt him?"

"I've got a pretty good idea about that, too. A damned good idea. And I'm going to keep on digging until I can prove it. So don't try anything, get me? If you do"— Kossmeyer drew a finger across his throat—"zip! Curtains.

It'll be the last goddamned thing you ever try."

He slid out of the booth, tossed a coin on the table and walked away. Dusty finished his cigarette, studying himself in the mirrored panels of the wall.

Nothing had changed. He was still as sure, inside and out, as when he had entered the restaurant. Kossmeyer had temporarily cracked his calm façade, but now the crevices were smoothly resealed.

The attorney had only been guessing, trying to frighten him. He realized that he could no longer get any money from Dusty—via his father—and the fact had enraged him. But there was nothing he could do.

He couldn't reveal the truth (rather, Dusty corrected himself, the seeming truth) about the petition. He couldn't possibly know what had motivated him, Dusty, to sign the petition. The motive—what *might* have been the motive— was gone. It had been buried, figuratively and literally, with her.

Confident and calm, he left the restaurant and drove home. As was frequently the case, Doctor Lane was just leaving the house when he arrived. The doctor had long since recovered from the exacted politeness of their one interview. Now, he was himself again, the self, at least, that he normally displayed to Dusty: irritable, brusque, virtually insulting.

How was Mr. Rhodes getting along? Well, he was getting along as well as could be expected, which was not, in Doctor Lane's opinion, very damned well.

"I've told you before, Rhodes," he said testily. "This is as much a morale problem as a physical one. Your father needs to feel wanted, that he's still of some importance. And no man can feel that way when he's forced to live and look like a tramp."

"He's not forced to," Dusty retorted. "I give him plenty of money to keep up his appearance. Anything he wants, within reason, I—"

"You do, eh? Within reason, eh?" The doctor gave him a cynical stare. "Well, you'd better start giving him a little more, get me? Be a little more reasonable. Do *something*, for God's sake! This is getting to be a disgrace."

He yanked the car door open, tossed his medicine kit

upon the seat. With an irritated scowl, he started around to the opposite door, then, whirled and stamped back to the bellboy.

"Yes?" he said, his face thrust almost against Dusty's "You said something to me, Rhodes?"

"I said," said Dusty, evenly, "that if you don't want to treat the case, I can call in another doctor."

"No"—Lane shook his head. "No," he said again, his voice muted to an icy purr. "I'll tell you what you can do, Rhodes. You can start taking better care of your father, or you can hire someone who will take care of him. Do I make myself clear? You can do it of your own free will, as a son should, or I'll take steps to compel you to." He hesitated, wet his lips, continued in a milder tone. After all, he'd been the Rhodes' family doctor for years. And he'd known this young man since he was a squirt in short pants. "Sure that, uh, nothing of that kind will be necessary," he went on. "I know your expenses have been pretty high, and it's hard for a man holding a full-time job to do much else. But, well, see what you can do about it, eh? Do the best you can."

Dusty promised that he certainly would. He was no more afraid of the doctor than he was of Kossmeyer, but there was no point in making an enemy of him. He needed friends; he was very apt to need them, at any rate. And— and the realization startled him—he had none. There were friends of the family, friends of his father. But there was none of his own. No one who could be depended upon to fight for him, stick up for him, if he got into trouble.

"I'll get busy on it right away," he promised. "I'm only sorry that you had to be bothered about such things, Doctor."

"Well. Well, that's all right," Lane said gruffly. "Know you've got the old man's welfare at heart—just a little thoughtless perhaps—or I wouldn't have said anything."

He drove away.

Entering the house, Dusty again sent Mr. Rhodes to the barber, again gathered up his clothes and called the laundry and cleaners. It would mean losing sleep today and still more tomorrow. But that would be the end of this particular difficulty. Kossmeyer was dropping his father's case. He would be making no more demands for money, and the old man would thus cease to filch from the household funds as he had been doing.

Dusty dialed the telephone, thinking of the attorney with sardonic amusement. That was always the way with these holier-than-thou guys, these guys who made such a show of standing on principles and to hell with the cost. They didn't care about money—oh, not at all!—but they never turned any down. They were too good to give you a decent word, to show a little understanding for you, but they weren't too good to take your money. If they couldn't get it in one way, they'd do it in another. Squeeze it out of someone close to you who was too trusting to see through them.

Kossmeyer must have known that Mr. Rhodes had no money of his own. He must have been aware that Dusty would not, or could not, have authorized the old man's steady and substantial expenditures. And yet—

Dusty frowned faintly, the smoothly satisfying chain of his thoughts temporarily unlinked. He didn't *know*, of course, that Kossmeyer had gotten any dough from his father. It would seem that he hadn't, in fact, since Mr. Rhodes had pestered him frequently to send the attorney a remittance. Then, well, then there was the way Kossmeyer had acted a few days ago: there in his office when the subject of fees had come up. He'd brushed it aside as something of no importance. In so many words, he'd offered to work for nothing. He'd been pretty sure, no doubt, that the offer would not be accepted, and, of course, a man as sharp as he was would know when to take it easy and when to put on the screws. But suppose . . . suppose he had really meant it. Suppose he hadn't received those hundreds of dollars, as much as fifteen or twenty dollars a week for more than a year.

Well—Dusty shrugged and resumed his telephoning—suppose he hadn't? What difference did it make whether the old man had simply wasted the money, let it get away from him, or whether he had given it to Kossmeyer?

He hung up the phone, and leaned back on the lounge. Fretfully, he lighted a cigarette and leaned forward again.

. . Hundreds of dollars, close to a thousand. And if Kossmeyer hadn't got it, who had? It didn't make any difference, of course—how could it?—but still it was damned puzzling. He couldn't push the riddle out of his mind.

Squandered? Wasted? Absently dribbled away or lost? The more he thought about it, the more preposterous the theory became. Mr. Rhodes had no vices, nothing he might have spent so much money on. Years of living on a modest salary had made him chronically frugal. He abhorred waste, and had demonstrated the fact frequently and recently. He was absent-minded, true, but not *that* absent-minded. On occasion, he might have forgotten his change from a purchase or lost a bill from his pocket. It was out of character, but he might have. But he would not have done so steadily, consistently, week after week.

There was only one explanation, then. Kossmeyer. The money had either gone to him, or it simply hadn't gone. And if it hadn't. . .

Dusty crushed out his cigarette, and stood up. Stepping to the screen door, he looked up and down the street. He stood there in the door for a moment, hesitant, feeling a faint twinge of shame. Then, he turned away purposefully, and entered his father's room.

It was as neat as the old man was unneat. The bed was made. The floor appeared to have been recently swept. A handful of toilet articles was tidily arranged on the dresser. Books stood in orderly array upon their several shelves.

He examined them, the books first. Riffling their pages, shaking them, hastily replacing them on the shelves. Next, after another look up and down the street, came the bed. He jerked off the covers, went over the mattress swiftly but carefully. There was nothing. No smallest slit, nor any place where the ticking had been restitched. He re-did the bed and moved to the dresser. In the bottom drawer he found a small steel file. He lifted it out, and raised the unlocked lid.

There was nothing here, either. Only old letters, old receipts, old and yellowed newspaper clippings. And a couple of old insurance policies. One, a thousand-dollar policy, carried a twenty-year-old date. The other—ten thousand dollars, double indennity—was dated some five years ago. Both, of course, named his mother as beneficiary. Both, consequently, would have long since lapsed.

He returned the file to the drawer. That completed his search of the room.

The following morning, having sent his father to a picture

show, he searched the rest of the house. His findings totaled a dime (under the bathtub) and three pennies (extricated from the cushions of the living-room furniture). That was all.

Well, he hadn't actually expected to turn up a horde. He'd been sure all along that Kossmeyer had got the money. He went to bed, more pleased than otherwise, glad that his opinion of the attorney had been positively confirmed.

He ate.
He slept.
He worked.

He conferred with Tug and his boys several times. He went to extraordinary pains to keep Mr. Rhodes presentable.

Eat, sleep, work: that was about the sum of his existence. It seemed that there should have been something more, but that was all.

The days, the nights, slipped by, blending uneventfully one with another. Almost abruptly the day came, *that* day.

Two-thirty in the morning of that day.

At midnight, politely but implacably, the Manton had begun urging its guests toward their rooms. Now, at two-thirty in the morning, with the coffee shop closed, the porters and elevator operator gone, the lobby was almost painfully quiet. It was as though no one had ever walked the sparkling marble floors, sat in the overstuffed chairs and divans. As though no one ever had or ever would. The cleanliness was so forbidding, the silence so sepulchral.

The silence was contagious; it pressed in on you, demanding silence. Up in the cashier's cage, Dusty unconsciously lowered his voice. Then, as Bascom squirmed on his stool, he raised it again.

Five-oh-five, Holloway. Food thirty-eight dollars, tips five, total forty-three. Bar twenty, tips three-fifty, total twenty-three fifty. Newsstand miscellaneous, twelve. C.O.D.'s fifty-two. Valet—"

"Let's see." Bascom held out his hand for the charge slips without turning around. "Hmmm. Living high, but he doesn't spend a nickel. Could be that he doesn't have it to spend."

"Could be," Dusty murmured.

"Well"—Bascom tossed the account to one side— "that's a headache for the day crew. Let's have the next one."

Dusty continued. Now and then he stole a look at the clerk. Bascom was strangely calm, matter-of-fact, tonight. Not friendly or unfriendly, simply a man carrying out a job that had to be done.

It was the way he should act, of course; everything had to go on as usual, right up until the time of the holdup. But Dusty wondered at his ability to do it. He, himself, was anything but calm. Now, here right at the last when he needed confidence most, it was suddenly draining away.

Dusty glanced at the lobby clock. Two-thirty sharp. What was holding them up? They—Tug and the two men who were in on the deal—should have started down the stairs at two-twenty. Ten minutes was more than enough time to get down to the lobby. So unless something had gone wrong. . .

Tug had warned him not to leave the cashier's cage after two-thirty. If there was a room call or an elevator signal at two-twenty-five, or even a minute or so later, fine. He was to take care of it, and get back to the cage as fast as he could. But after that, no. People couldn't expect prompt service at this hour of the morning. If they did comment on the fact later, nothing could be made of it. The robbery would have been going on, and—

But it wasn't going on! It was two-thirty-four, well, two-thirty-three, and nothing had happened. Suppose he got a room call, or the elevator night-bell rang, now. Suppose he stalled on it, and Tug and his boys didn't show up until three. How would he be able to explain that? And how could he cover up, meanwhile, with Bascom? Bascom wasn't supposed to know that he was in on the robbery. And Bascom certainly would suspect the truth, if he stalled indefinitely. A few minutes, yes: while they finished a transcript sheet or a series of charges. But a few minutes had already passed—it was already two thirty—and. . . Where were they? *For God's sake, where were they?*

"Bill. . ." Bascom spoke with his back still turned. "You made a bad mistake, Bill."

"W-What?" Dusty plunged out of fear and into terror. "W-when? H-how do you—?"

"You've been making a lot of mistakes. You don't know what you're doing. Why don't you go home? I can say that you took sick, and call for another boy."

What was he talking about? The work or the other? Did he know or. . . ?

"Do it, Bill. Now. Before you make a really big mistake."

"I—*No!*" Dusty gasped. "I mean, I'm all right I—"

"You're all wrong. But if you leave now, you can still. . ." Bascom paused, leaving the sentence unfinished. For from somewhere, up there on the echoing darkness of the mezzanine, a door had creaked open, and now there was the rapid *pad-pad* of feet upon thick carpeting. And then the clatter of those same feet descending the marble steps to the lobby.

They came down in a group, almost on each other's heels. One of them hurried up the lobby to the front door, another took up a position at the taxi entrance. And the third, Tug Trowbridge, stopped at the cashier's cage.

Something dropped to the desk from his hand, tinkled faintly. Six—no, seven tiny keys. The same hand grasped Bascom by the shirt front, hauled him up against the opening. The other thrust a gun into the clerk's chest.

"All right, kid," he snapped. "Get busy!"

"B-but—" Dusty stared at him, stupefied. This wasn't the way it was supposed to be. Tug had promised to keep him in the clear, with nothing to do but—

"Goddammit, move! Get the ledger and the other keys. Get them boxes out here!"

Dusty's head was swimming. He stammered, "B-but you s-said—"

"You heard what I said! Now, do it!"

He couldn't do it. He couldn't even move. Then his eyes moved from the gangster to Bascom, and he couldn't see him full-face, but what he saw was enough. Bascom was startled, too. For him also things were not going as they had been planned.

"You hear me, Dusty? I have to tell you one more god-damned time, and—"

And Dusty sprang into action.

He had left the platform. The plunge was over, and now there was nothing but the short easy swim to shore. This was as it should be. As he must have known it would be. He hadn't known, of course, or certainly he wouldn't have agreed to it. He'd had no idea of the real truth. But so long as it was this way. . .

He sank deeper and deeper into the water; its pressure was unbearable. And then he was on the bottom—absolute bottom. And amazingly the pressure was gone. Once he surrendered to it fully, ceased to resist, there was no more.

Sure, he'd known; and he knew what must certainly happen after this. And what the hell of it? All that mattered now was getting to shore. . .getting away with it.

Swiftly, he unlocked seven of the little vault doors, yanked out their long steel boxes. He placed them on the desk, to one side of Bascom, and Tug gave him a tight-lipped grin of approval.

"Atta boy! Now, reach around him, kid—I got the bag under my coat—and. . . Swell. You're doing fine. Now stuff the dough into it, and—"

"What about a count on it?"

"Count!" Tug let out a surprised grunt, then chuckled softly. "A real pro, ain't he, Bask?" *Bascom was silent.* "A good idea, kid, but make it fast. Just riffle through it. Don't matter if you're a grand or two off."

Dusty nodded. He flipped back the lid of the first box, turned through the thick sheaf of bills. They were all hundreds and fifties, with a preponderance of the latter. Large enough to total high without bulk, small enough for easy negotiation.

"Twenty-seven thousand." He glanced at Tug. "Okay?"

"Yeah, yeah! For Christ's sake, Dusty!"

There was twenty-four thousand, five hundred in the

next box. The third held thirty-eight thousand, fifty. The fourth. . .

All together there was two hundred and thirty-two thousand. Approximately that much. Tug nodded impatiently as he repeated the figure.

"Yeah, hell. It's close enough anyway. . . . Now, you remember the combo on that bag? One turn right from zero, back left to ten, right to forty, and then left to—"

"I know. All the way, ten, forty, thirty. . . What about your own box, here? Haven't you got—?"

Tug cursed shakily. "Jesus Christ! Forget it, will you? Just get the thing checked and get back here!"

Dusty snapped the bag shut, spun the knob of the combination lock. He unlocked the cage, and hurried down the long counter, snatching up the checkroom key from the bell captain's stand.

He emerged from behind the counter, turned into the alcove which bordered one side of the check stand. The baggage-receiving space opened onto that. He unlocked its long window, vaulted the brass-surfaced counter, and turned on the light switch.

Two cigar boxes were nailed to the wall immediately below the switch. Dusty took a rubber band from one, and an orange-colored oblong of pasteboard from another. He affixed a check to the bag, shredded its stub into a wastebasket, took a long look at the number as he slid the bag onto the shelf. *Four, nine, nine, four. Forty-nine, ninety-four.* Forty-nine and reverse. That would be easy to remember.

He switched off the light, vaulted back over the counter, relocked the window. Hurrying back down into the lobby, swift but sure of himself, unpanicked, he heard the ringing of the bell captain's phone. And yards away he saw the alarm on Tug's face, and the sudden uneasiness of the two men at the doors. Why, they were jumpy. *They* were, and he was not. He was grinning secretly, patronizingly, as he entered and locked the door of the cashier's cage.

Everything was all right. It was exactly eight minutes since Tug had thrust his gun into Bascom's ribs. How much better could they want it?

"That goddamned phone, Dusty! Maybe you ought to—"

"Huh-uh. The operator will figure I'm busy. She'll stop,

and call back in a few minutes."

"You sure? She won't—" The ringing stopped, but Tug still looked anxious.. "She won't call someone, tell 'em that she—"

Dusty shook his head. "What's the difference, anyway? It's all over, isn't it?"

"Well . . . well, yeah," said Tug, almost wonderingly. I guess it just about is, kid."

"Bill!" Bascom spoke for the first time. "Listen to me, Bill! It doesn't matter about me, but you've got to prom—"

Tug's gun exploded. Bascom reeled backward, clutching his chest, and Tug fired again. And again. The clerk's body jerked. Slowly, it began to bend at the waist. It sagged down and down, and he was clawing at his chest, now, gasping and clawing—a terrible rattle in his throat. Then, his knees swayed and crumpled, and blood gushed from his mouth, and he pitched forward to the floor.

The rattling ceased. He lay silent, motionless.

"All right, kid"— Tug's gun swerved and pointed at Dusty. "Here's your story. . ."

He spoke swiftly. He said, "Got it?" And then, "Now, just take it easy—we got to make this look good—but just take it easy and—"

And he fired again.

Dusty screamed. He staggered and went down, on top of Bascom's body.

Instinctively, he had tried to dodge the bullet, and the attempt came close to being fatal. Tug's aim was thrown off. The bullet went into Dusty's arm at an angle, and creased a furrow across his ribs. He was not seriously injured but he might have been. It looked as though Tug had tried to kill him.

So now he was a hero, above dispute and suspicion. A plucky young man who had tried to wrest a loaded gun from a murderer's grasp. The newspapers carried daily reports on his condition. The hotel, in addition to paying his hospital bills, had given him a check for three hundred dollars. Detectives had taken him back and forth through his story repeatedly, but they were respectful, apologetic, about it. They were at a dead end in the case, had been almost from the beginning. And they had to go through the motions of doing something.

A detective was with him today, the last of his nine days in the hospital. He had just happened to be in the neighborhood, he explained, rather abashedly. So if Dusty wouldn't mind, since he'd be going home tomorrow and they wouldn't be bothering him any more. . .

Dusty felt a little sorry for him. He said it was no bother at all. "I don't think I've overlooked or forgotten anything, but I might have."

"Well. . . Now about the time, then. Were you and Bascom always in the cashier's cage at two-thirty?"

"Almost always. Of course, I might have a bell—a call—or Bascom might have to leave for a minute. But we'd almost always be there at that time."

"Why that particular time instead of some other?"

"It was the quietest part of the shift, for one thing. We weren't so apt to be interrupted. Also, there'd seldom be any room charges after that time. If we tried to do it before that, while the coffee shop was still open and a lot of people were still up—"

"Uh-huh, sure. But what about the tag end of your shift, say up between six and seven in the morning? You'd start getting more charges, then, wouldn't you?"

"A few. Bascom would put them on the room accounts as fast as they came."

"Why didn't you do them all at once? If you'd done that, held up your cashier work until there were other people around. . ." The detective broke off with a sheepish look. "How stupid can I get, huh? I ask you why you don't do something when you'd'd've been too busy to do it."

"That's right." Dusty smiled sympathetically. "I wouldn't have had time to help. Bascom would have been busy with people checking in and out."

"Yeah, sure," the detective nodded. "Now, what did you think when you saw Tug and his two thugs heading down the stairs? Didn't that strike you as pretty screwy? I know he was paying the hotel big money and he'd never caused any trouble before. But two-thirty in the morning—three guys hiking down nine flights of stairs at two-thirty in the morning—you must have—"

"It's like I told you," Dusty said. "I figured that the night-bell on the elevator must have gone out of order. They'd signaled and when I didn't come with the car they'd walked down."

"But what would they be doing up at that hour, anyway? I know you told me, but it just don't seem like—"

"I'm afraid it's about all I can tell you. We were used to seeing Tug up late. He usually came in late, with a couple of his men, and sometimes he came back down stairs with them when they left."

"Well"—the detective sighed and leaned back in his chair. Then, he straightened up suddenly. "Wait a minute! You say you figured the elevator bell was out of order. But if that had been the case he'd have called you, wouldn't he? When the elevator didn't come he'd have telephoned downstairs from his room?"

Dusty hesitated. It was a point that had been overlooked until now. "You're right," he said. "I should have thought of that. But I just wasn't suspicious of Tug like I might have been of some people, and there wasn't any time to think. I saw him and those fellows coming down the stairs. The next thing I knew, he'd grabbed Bascom and shoved a gun in his ribs. All I could think of was that I'd better do what he said or he'd kill Bascom."

"Uh-uh, sure." The detective sighed again. "Now what was it Tug said there at the last, just before he pulled the trigger on Bascom?"

"He said, Here's your share. Or maybe it was, Here's your cut."

"And that didn't register on you, either? It didn't occur to you that Bascom must have been working with Tug?"

"Look. Officer"— Dusty spread his hands. "Here's a man I've waited on for more than a year, a man who's always been friendly, a star guest of the hotel. And suddenly he holds us up, and shoots the man I'm working with. All within the space of a few minutes. You don't do much reasoning at a time like that. Maybe you would, but—"

"Okay, okay," the detective said hastily. "I didn't mean to sound like I was faulting you, Mr. Rhodes. You were a lot more clear-headed than most people would have been, showed a hell of a lot more guts. Me, I can't see myself making a grab for that gun."

"Well," Dusty smiled engagingly, "I probably wouldn't do it again either. I was just scared, I suppose, afraid I was going to get killed next."

"And you weren't far wrong at that." The detective shook his head, frowning. "That Bascom—y'know, I just can't figure him. Even if Tug had shot square with him, he must have known that he'd be on a spot. We'd investigate him, and find out about his record. The hotel had already got a letter about him—you know about that, I guess—and—"

"But they didn't pay much attention to it. Bascom had worked there for years, and he'd never given them any reason to suspect him. One anonymous letter wouldn't have counted much against a record like his."

"Yeah. Well, maybe not then. Maybe we wouldn't have checked on him. The way he thought the deal was going to be, it would have left him looking pretty good. Tug grabs him before he knows what's happening. He doesn't even touch the boxes himself. So maybe. . ."

His voice wandered on absently, aimlessly, a dull probe seeking the non-existent. And a sudden hunch sprang into Dusty's mind.

If his and Bascom's roles had been reversed, if he had been killed and if Bascom had quoted Tug as saying 'Here's your cut. . .'

Why not? A bellboy was about as low down the ladder as you could get, while a night clerk was a minor executive. His story would have been believed. He would have been the hero, and Dusty the dead villain. . . Doubtless, Bascom had believed it would be that way. And, doubtless— perhaps— Had Tug planned it that way in the beginning?

It wasn't nice to think about. There was no sense in thinking about it, and there were much more pleasant things to dwell upon. Marcia Hillis, for example, and fifty per cent of two hundred and thirty-two thousand dollars.

"Well"—the detective stood up. "Guess I'd better be running along. If you should happen to think of anything, why. . ."

"I don't know what it would be but I'll certainly let you know."

"Fine. Appreciate it." He turned dispiritedly toward the door, a big man with sagging shoulders and a tired gray face. "Oh, yeah," he paused. "Guess I didn't tell you, did I? We found those guys that were with Tug."

"Found them! W-what—?"

"Uh-huh. In the river. Tied together with bailing wire. Looks like they'd been there since the night of the hold up."

"W-well"— Dusty swallowed. "Why. . . What do you suppose—?"

"Tug, of course. To beat them out of their split. Seems like they should have figured on it, and given it to him instead. But, well, that's the way things go."

He left.

Dusty walked over to the window, pulling his bathrobe around him. So Tug's boys had got it, too. Tug had double-crossed them, just as he had Bascom. And what about it, anyway? What difference did it make? Tug wouldn't double-cross *him*, because he damned well couldn't, and that was all that mattered.

He'd be out of the hospital tomorrow. In a few days, as soon as his shoulder limbered up a little more, he'd be back to work. Then, the split of the money—Tug would get in touch with him about that—and then. . .

He turned away from the window. He sank down into an easy chair and leaned back, propping his feet up on the bed. The money. He still didn't know how Tug planned to collect his share. The gangster had impatiently pointed out that they'd have to wait and see, that circumstances following the robbery would dictate arrangements. And that was true, of course; it was just about the way it had to be. But still—hadn't he been pretty offhand about it? Had he been concealing something on this point as he had on the other?

Well. . .Dusty shrugged, dismissing the idea. That didn't matter either. Tug could only get to the money through him. There was no way that Tug could do him out of his share. That was the important thing, so to hell with details.

. . . A nurse brought his dinner on a tray. He ate leisurely and read the evening papers. There was a brief item about his leaving the hospital tomorrow. There was a long story about the discovery of the murdered gangsters. He laid the papers aside, yawning, and glanced at his wristwatch.

He had told his father not to visit him tonight, since it was his last night here, and he hoped to God that he wouldn't. Not that the old man hadn't looked presentable on his nightly visits, but—well, he'd just rather not scare him. His concern made Dusty uncomfortable. His presence was a reminder of a perplexing and seemingly insoluble problem. Dusty just couldn't think when his father was around. There was a stumbling block in his mind, an obscuring shadow over the pleasant picture of his thoughts.

Marcia Hillis was working with Tug. He had become more and more sure of that fact. He was also sure of his attraction for her—*strange how very sure he was of that.* And now that her work with Tug was done, now that he had money, it would only be a matter of time until they were together.

That was the way it would be. It was the way it *had* to be. It wasn't just wishful thinking—by God, it wasn't! He had lost her once, lost the only woman in the world. And, now, miraculously, she had reappeared, she had come back into the aching emptiness of his life. And this time, this time, he would not let her get away.

He would have her. It was unthinkable that he might not. In his mind, the possession was already accomplished; they were already together, he and Marcia Hillis, delighting in one another, delighting one another. And there was no room in the picture for his father. With his father, there was no picture.

How could he explain her to the old man? How could he explain the money? He wouldn't have to explain right away, of course. It would be months before he dared quit the hotel and move on to another city—another country. But the time would come. Or, rather, it would never come, as long as his father lived.

As long as he lived. . .

Dusty had no visitors that night. In the morning, the doctor gave him a final examination and a nurse brought his clothes. He took an elevator downstairs. Unused to exercise, he wobbled a little as he started across the lobby to the street. And a soft hand closed over his arm.

"Let me help you, Mr. Rhodes," said Marcia Hillis.

He wasn't surprised, merely startled for the moment. He had been expecting to see her, and her appearance there, as he was leaving the hospital, virtually explained the reason behind it. She wasn't quite through with her assignment with Tug. There was one more thing to be done. He knew what it was, and how it was to be done, almost before she said a word.

They took a cab to his house. She assisted him inside, was received with absent matter-of-factness by the old man. He was glad, he said, that Bill had hired her. They would need someone, with Bill just out of the hospital, and he himself wasn't much help he guessed.

"Now, nonsense, Dad!" Dusty was almost exuberant in his happiness. "You do a lot more than you should. I've been meaning to get someone in before this to make things easier for you."

"Well, now," Mr. Rhodes beamed. "I—that's certainly nice of you, son."

"You must have had a hard time while I was gone. So today you get a vacation. Go to a good show, get yourself a good meal; just take it easy and enjoy yourself."

He pressed a ten-dollar bill upon Mr. Rhodes. He saw him out the door, watched for a moment as he trudged down the walk toward the bus stop. That would take care of the old nuisance. It was worth ten times ten dollars to get rid of him for a while.

He was on the point of saying as much when he turned back around, but the look on Marcia's face stopped him. There was a tenderness in her eyes, a warmth in her expression, that he had never seen before.

"You know," she said softly, "I think I like you."

"Think?"

"Mmmm," she said, and laughed. "And I think I'd like some coffee, too. So if you'll introduce me to your kitchen, show me where you keep things . . ."

She made coffee, donning an apron he gave her. He watched her, dreamily, as she moved about the kitchen, drinking in every delicious detail of her. The hair, the compactly curving body, the clothes, the—The clothes. He couldn't be sure of it, but she seemed to be dressed the same as she had been the last time he'd seen her.

She turned around suddenly, surprising him in his looking. She said, "Yes? Something on your mind, Dusty?" And he hastily shook his head.

"I was just wondering about your clothes. I mean, you'll be here for some time and . . ."

"Oh," she shrugged. "Well, I'll pick my baggage up in a day or two. It wasn't convenient this morning."

She set the coffee on the table, and sat down across from him. Hand trembling a little, he lifted the cup. Reaction was setting in; he at last felt surprise—wonder at this incredibly wondrous happening. She was actually here! They were really together. And, of course, he had known that they would be, but now that they were . . .

He had to put down the coffee cup. Fingers fumbling, he managed to light a cigarette and hold a match for hers. She smiled sympathetically, steadying his hand with her own.

"You don't have your strength back yet, Dusty. Why don't you lie down for a while?"

"I'm all right. We've got a lot to talk about, and—"

"You can lie down and talk. Come on, now, before you wear yourself out completely."

She guided him into his bedroom. He stretched out on the bed, and she sat down at his side.

"Well, Dusty . . ." She smoothed the hair back from his forehead. "You didn't seem very surprised to see me today."

"I wasn't. I was pretty sure you must be working with Tug."

"You were? And how did that make you feel about me, Dusty, about being tricked into—?"

"It didn't change anything. I figured you were probably in the same boat I was in. You were on a spot, and you had to follow orders."

"Did you, Dusty?" She squeezed his hand. "I'm glad you

understood. Some day I'll tell you how it was, but—"

"It doesn't matter. I—nothing mattered but you. Right from the first time I saw you."

The statement sounded awkwardly blunt, a little ridiculous. But she smiled gravely, obviously pleased.

"I'm glad, Dusty. Because, you see . . . well, I rather felt the same way. It was the way you acted, I guess, as though you'd been waiting for me, expecting me. I felt like you were someone I'd known a long time ago, and— Oh, I don't know," she laughed. "Anyway, I don't suppose a girl should admit such things, should she?"

"Yes!" he exclaimed. "I mean—I don't mean you should—"

"I know what you mean, Dusty. I know."

She bent down, pressing her mouth against his. Then, as his arms went around her, she slid firmly out of his embrace.

"Not now, darling. I hope there will be more later—a great deal more. But, now, I don't know."

"But why?" He started to sit up, and she pushed him back down. "You said you liked me, felt the same way as I did. I'll have plenty of money, and—"

"The money isn't too important to me, Dusty. Not nearly as much, I'm afraid, as it is to you. I like it, yes, but I've never had a great deal and I've gotten along all right without it. I could keep right on getting along without it. I wonder if you could."

"But I—we won't have to!"

"Won't we? That money won't last forever, no more than ten years, say, if we're only mildly extravagant. What would you do when it's gone?"

"Well, I—" He shook his head impatiently. "What would anyone do? Marcia, I—"

"Not anyone. You. I'm quite a bit older than you are, Dusty. I won't be young ten years from now, but you will. How would you feel then—broke and saddled with a middle-aged woman? What would you do about it?"

"What?" he frowned. "I—look, Marcia. I want you to marry me, not just—"

"I hoped you did. But that still doesn't answer my question. What happens when my looks are gone, and the money's gone? Would there still be something left for you, something more important than money or appearances? I'd have to be sure of that, Dusty. I have to know you better than I do now."

"I . . . I don't know what you mean," he said slowly. "I don't see what you're driving at."

"Murder, mainly. Murderers. If a man kills to get himself out of one unpleasant situation, he'll do it again."

She nodded calmly, staring down at him in the shade-drawn dimness, and a cold chill raced up Dusty's spine. He was suddenly conscious of the room's quiet, of their isolation here.

"B-but—" He gulped. "But I haven't killed anyone!"

"Not actually, perhaps, but technically. You knew Bascom was going to be killed!"

"But I didn't? Tug didn't tell me a thing about it. He told me—told me that no one would be hurt."

"And you believed him?"

"Why not? I didn't know anything about things like that. All I knew was that you were in trouble, that you might get killed if I didn't do what Tug told me to."

"That isn't what you said a moment ago. You said you knew I was working with Tug."

"Not at the time. Even afterwards, I wasn't positive. I— Who are you to talk, anyway? You got me into the deal. If it hadn't been for you, I—"

"Would it have made any difference, Dusty? You don't think you might have been in it anyway?"

"How could I have been? What do you mean? Dammit"—he sat up, scowling. "I could ask some questions myself. What about you knowing that Bascom was going to be killed? You quiz me about it when you must have known yourself that—"

"I didn't. If I had, I'd hardly be concerned about your being involved."

"Well, I didn't know either."

"I hope not, Dusty. I want to believe that you didn't. So let's not discuss it any more now, shall we not? Give me a little more time, tell me how we're going to get the money out of the hotel, and then—well, we'll see then."

"But, why? What's there to—?"

"Why not? We'll have to wait anyway. We've just met, supposedly. You'll have to go on working at the hotel."

"Yes, but—but, Marcia . . ."

He broke off, unable to say what he had intended to, to point out the incongruity of the situation. She was in this thing as deeply as he, she was closer to Tug apparently than he was. She'd been around—she damned well had to know what the score was. So why then all this squeamishness? Why all the fuss about Bascom's death?

It didn't add up. Even taking that older-than-you-are, what-about-the-future stuff at its face value it didn't fit together. So maybe they had to be careful for a while. Maybe it was logical for her to go slow on tying herself up permanently. But they were alone now, and she'd been around from way back. And yet he couldn't even give her a feel without—

"Oh," she said, and it was as though he had spoken the thought aloud. "I see, Dusty, and I don't blame you. I haven't been everything I should be, and—"

"Nuts, nonsense," he said quickly. "Now about the money. Come around to the hotel any time after I go on duty, a little after twelve, say. You want to get something out of a suitcase you've left in the checkroom—a lot of people do that—and—"

"I understand. I supposed you'd do it that way."

"Well, uh—that's all there is to it, then."

She nodded, went on looking at him. At last she said absently, "Perhaps we shouldn't wait. Perhaps it would be better now, since you feel as you do. Since it's so important—or unimportant."

"Now, wait a minute!" His face flushed. "I haven't said anything! My God, you can't blame me for wanting to—to—"

"I don't. Nor for thinking what you think."

She got up and left the room. He heard the front door close, and the snap of the lock, and then she was back again.

She toed off one shoe, then the other. Quite casually, she unfastened the snaps of her dress, slipped it up and over her head. The slip came next. Then—then the other things. All that remained.

And then she stretched out at his side. And waited.

He was too startled to move for a moment; it had all happened so swiftly. Then, his senses responded to the wonderful reality of her, and he moaned and . . .

She lay supine, docile, under his hungrily groping hands. They roamed over her body unhindered, nothing forbidden nor withheld. And her mouth received his in long, breathtaking kisses. It was almost too much, more ecstasy than he could bear. To have her at last, after all these years of hunger and hopelessness, to have this—the impossible dream come true—his for the taking.

He moaned again. He turned, pulling her body under his and then he opened his eyes. Looked into hers.

"What—what's the matter?" he said.

"You mean," she said, "you're not enjoying yourself?"

"Look. If you didn't want to, why—?"

"I though I explained. To see how important this was to you—how much value or little value you placed on it."

"But that—that's crazy! What does it prove? For God's sake, Marcia, you can't—"

"To me, it proves a great deal. To you—well, I'm waiting to find out."

"B-but—" But it was impossible, unbearable! He couldn't stop now. Jesus, he couldn't! He *couldn't!* But if he didn't . . .

He bit his lip. Suddenly, he thrust himself up, dropped down panting at her side. And he lay there, eyes clenched, trembling from the terrible effort. It was all right now. He was exhausted, now, drained dry of strength—weak as he was disappointed.

Her arm went around his neck, pulling his head against her breast. She held it there, gently, stroking his hair.

"You'll be glad, darling," she whispered. "You'll see. You'll be so glad you waited."

"All right," he said. "I . . . all right."

"You don't hate me, do you, darling? Please don't. No matter what I—how I act. Because I won't be doing it to hurt you. I love you and I want you to love me, to keep on loving me, and if we don't get started off right . . ."

"All right," he repeated. "I said it was all right, didn't I?"

"And I said you'd be glad," she whispered. "And you will . . ."

Although there was still some soreness in his shoulder, he went back to work two days later. He wanted to get the pay-off made and over with. He wanted to—had to—get away from his father. For, that first day excepted, the old man had hardly left the house. And when he did leave on some errand, he was back within minutes.

He was always hovering around Marcia, offering to do things for her, inquiring about her comfort. He was always underfoot, butting into their conversations, making a thoroughgoing pest of himself. He stayed up at night until they retired. If they went to the kitchen to fix coffee, or out the porch for a breath of air, he tagged along. They couldn't get rid of him. Marcia, for her part, showed no desire to.

Once Dusty did manage to get her alone for a few minutes, and he made some sarcastic remark about the old man. She looked at him sharply.

"Why Dusty," she laughed, half-frowning. "What a thing to say about your own father! He's just been very lonely, that's all. Surely, you don't begrudge—"

"Oh, hell," he snapped. "I've been here right along, haven't I? Why would he be lonely?"

"Yes," she said. "Why would he be?"

He smoothed over the incident, told her laughingly that he guessed he was just jealous. And after that he went out of his way to be pleasant to Mr. Rhodes. But the effort told on his nerves. If he had to keep it up one more day, he felt— just one more day—he'd crack up.

She came out to his car with him the night he returned to work. It was dark, moonless. There was a threat of storm in the heavy, overheated air. She kissed him, remained within the circle of his arms for a moment.

"A little after twelve, then, darling?"

"Or later. Whenever Dad goes to sleep."

"I come to the side entrance in a taxi," she recited. "I have the taxi wait and come inside. If you're not there, I speak to the clerk and he'll have me wait until you return. I— He will, won't he, Dusty? He wouldn't offer to open the checkroom himself?"

"Not a chance. It would be beneath him, see, bellboy's work, and it would make me sore. He'd be cheating me out of a tip."

She nodded, still clinging to him. He bent his head a little and touched his lips to the sweet-smelling hair.

"About Tug, Marcia. I haven't asked before, and I don't want you to tell me if you'd—"

"It's a dangerous secret, darling; it could be one. There's nothing to be gained by your knowing, and everything to lose."

"Well"—he hesitated. "But is it safe for you? You know where Tug is. Once you give him the money, he might figure that—"

"I won't give it to him. I'm going to leave it in a certain place where he can get it. Don't worry, Dusty." She patted his cheek, lovingly. "Everything's going to be all right."

They kissed again, stood whispering together a moment longer. At last she stepped back, and he reached for the door of the car. A streak of heat lightning raced across the sky. He paused on the point of sliding into the seat.

"Your clothes," he said. "Want me to drive you in tomorrow, and pick them up?"

"Clothes? Oh, yes. Maybe that would be a good idea."

"Well. Anything else? Sure you can get all the dough in that bag of yours?"

He knew that she could. It was an outsize shoulder bag, and she would remove the contents before coming to the hotel. She nodded absently to the question but she continued to stand there at the curb, a small frown on her heart-shaped face.

He glanced at the radiant dial of the dashboard clock. Nine-fifteen, and he was supposed to be in uniform by ten tonight. They were taking his picture for the morning papers.

"I've got to run, Marcia. Is there something else— anything bothering you?"

"We-el. . . Oh, I guess not," she laughed ruefully. "I don't think I should mention it, anyway."

"Why not?"

"Because. It just isn't my place to suggest it. After all, it must have already occurred to you, and as long as you haven't said anything. . ."

"About what? What are you— Oh," he said slowly. "Well. . ." And his voice trailed off into an uncomfortable pause.

Actually, he had thought very little about it, how he was going to get his share of the money out of the hotel. A problem so simple required little thought. Unlike Tug, he had unlimited time. He could take months at the task, carrying it out in his wallet a few hundreds at a shift. It was the easiest way and the safest way. The Manton's bellboys made good money. No suspicion would attach to one with a mere few hundred in his possession.

He explained this to her, and she nodded her understanding. There was no sign of resentment or hurt in the upturned face. Still, however, his discomfort grew: he felt awkward, constrained to go on explaining. And the more he said—logical as it was—the worse it sounded.

It might be difficult to open the money satchel, take out Tug's share and transfer it to her bag. It could certainly be done, all right, but there might be difficulties. The safest and simplest thing to do would be to give her the satchel itself, with *all* the money.

And why not do it? Let her hold Tug's share *and* his.

Why not, unless. . .

She touched his arm gently. "I understand, darling. Now, run along and don't think anything more about it."

"It's not"—he hesitated—"I wouldn't want you to think I didn't trust you. It's just that I'd planned it the other way, and—"

"Of course." She urged him into the car, closed the door after him. "Why wouldn't you trust me? After all, you're practically trusting me with your life."

"Well. . . well," he murmured, feebly. "I'll, uh, see you, then."

He drove to the hotel, downcast, feeling that he had acted like a suspicious fool. He decided—half-decided—to give her the satchel when she came that night. Why not? Either she was completely trustworthy or she was not to be trusted at all. If Tug's money could be trusted to her, then so could his own.

Or couldn't it? Why couldn't it be?

Frowning, he buttoned his uniform jacket, adjusted the wing tips of his shirt collar. *Why?* Well, there was one reason. One hideous, heart-wrenching reason. She might not be finished with Tug after the pay-off, nor he with her. She might be much more to Tug then she pretended to be. And if she was—well, she had pointed it out herself. A hundred and sixteen thousand dollars wouldn't last forever; it would be gone in a few years. But with two hundred and thirty-two thousand. . .

Furiously, Dusty pushed the terrible thought out of his mind. No! A thousand times no; she couldn't be Tug's woman. She was *his*. She liked to be, and she was. And just to prove it—to prove his complete faith in her—he would give her the satchel tonight.

Maybe. Probably. Surely. Unless he thought of some really *good* reason for not doing it.

He finished dressing and left the locker room. Tolliver, the superintendent of service, and Steelman, the manager, were waiting for him in the latter's office. Tolliver called to the two photographers in the reception room. They sauntered in and set up their equipment.

The first pose was of Dusty shaking hands with the manager, while Tolliver looked on beaming. Then he posed between the two men, each with a hand on his shoulder. Finally, he was photographed by himself, arms folded in the traditional manner of bellboys "standing post."

Repeatedly, he had to be reminded to smile. Toward the last, the photographers became quite sharp with him, and the two executives were showing signs of annoyance.

Dusty returned to the locker room for a brief, pre-work smoke. His lips twisted in silent mimicry, *Lets see a smile Rhodes—a SMILE DAMMIT—don't you know how to smile?* And scowling he hurled away the cigarette, and started up the steps. To hell with them. To hell with the hotel. She would take his dough out tonight with Tug's, and the sooner they fired him after that, the better. The money would be waiting for him when he got home in the morning—she and the money. And as soon as he figured out an angle on the old man, how to shake the old bastard without causing trouble. . .

That was the way it would be. It would—could—be that way if he was sure of her.

Preoccupied, now and then frowning unconsciously, he began the night's duties. A few minutes before midnight, he went behind the keyrack and manipulated a series of light switches.

"And just what," said a chilly voice at his elbow, "do you think you are doing?"

Dusty jumped, startled. It was Mr. Fillmore, the night clerk hired to replace Bascom. He had come from a smaller, second-rate hotel, and the Manton was a big step upward for him. Unsure of himself, fearful that his authority might be infringed upon, he made a point of appearing the opposite. He knew his job, by golly. He was in charge here, not some smart-alecky bellboy.

"I asked you what you were doing," he repeated. "Who told you to fool around with those lights?"

Dusty explained curtly; he had taken an immediate dislike to the clerk. "We always do this at midnight, dim the lobby and light up the—"

"But it's not midnight yet. Won't be for five minutes. You put those lights back on, understand? When I want them off, I'll tell you."

"I've got a better idea than that," said Dusty. "Do it yourself."

Turning on his heel, he left the desk area. He kept his back turned as the clerk emerged from behind the key-rack and spoke to him sharply across the counter.

"We may as well get this clear right now, Rhodes. The hotel appreciates what you did, and they've shown that appreciation, but you're still a bellboy. While you're at work you have no more rights or privileges than any other bellboy. It—uh—it has to be that way, understand? I'm sure that Mr. Tolliver or Mr. Steelman will bear me out. I hope— I'm certain, of course—that it will never be necessary for me to report—"

"Go ahead," Dusty grunted, still not looking around. "Go ahead and report me and see what they say."

"Well, uh—" Fillmore cleared his throat—"well, now, I

wouldn't want to do that. Not at all. Sure we're going to
get along fine, now that this little misunderstanding is
cleared up, and. . ."

He left the sentence unfinished, moving up the counter
to the room-clerk section. He busied himself there, coldly
furious, angry as only the self-fearful can be when character
and circumstance conspire to make them ridiculous. . .
He'd been in the right, hadn't he? But that smart-aleck—
he'd acted snooty from the minute he stepped on the floor
tonight—had gotten gay with him. Crowded him into saying things that he hadn't meant to say. Well, maybe, certainly, he couldn't do anything about this. He'd look
foolish if he tried. But just wait! Something else would
come up. He'd put that young punk in his place yet!

There was a squeal of brakes at the side entrance.
Instantly, Fillmore arose from his stool, stood briskly alert
as a woman got out of the cab and came through the double
doors to the lobby. She ascended the three steps from the
foyer, paused for a moment in the muted glow of one of the
huge chandeliers. Fillmore gaped, his fearful fussy old
heart missing a beat. He'd never seen a woman who looked
like that. She was so beautiful that it almost hurt to look at
her. He hoped she didn't want a room. He'd have to turn
her down, of course, a woman alone at this time of night,
and he could see that she was a lady. As much a lady as she
was beautiful.

Gratefully, he noted that the cab was waiting for her. (She
didn't want a room, then.) Jealously, he watched as she
started across the lobby and Rhodes stepped forward to
meet her. Now there was presumption for you. There was
sheer gall. Accosting a lady—asking if *he* could help her—
instead of allowing her to proceed to the desk!

Fillmore's eyes glinted. He moved down the desk quickly,
leaned over the counter.

"Yes, madam?" he called. "Can I be of service to you?"
Rhodes whirled around, frowning. *That would show him, by
golly!* The lady looked momentarily surprised, then smiled
at him warmly.

"Could you, please? I left a bag here recently when I
checked out of the hotel. I see that your checkroom's
closed, but I wonder if—"

"Certainly. The boy will get it for you." Fillmore
snapped his fingers. "Front, boy! Get the lady's bag out of
the checkroom."

He slapped the key upon the counter. Rhodes snatched it
up, tight-lipped, strode down the lobby and rounded the
corner of the corridor to the checkroom window. The lady
followed him after a gracious smile at Fillmore.

The clerk grinned to himself. He flicked an invisible speck
of dust from his suit, silently crying down the small voice of
his conscience. Petty? A show-off? Nonsense. This was a
smart hotel—a real swell place. And its executives, and, by
golly, he was an executive!, were supposed to conduct
themselves accordingly. Maybe it wasn't absolutely necessary here at night, so much spit and polish, but he would
never be criticized for it. It was a kind of bonus. He was giving more than was expected of him.

Fillmore's bony hands clenched and unclenched, exult-
antly. So perhaps he couldn't complain about Rhodes . . .
not unless he did something completely out of the way. But
neither could Rhodes complain about him. He wouldn't get
very far, by golly, if he tried. He could keep that smart-aleck
on his toes all night long, make him toe the line. And
Rhodes would have to take it or else. If he rebelled, refused
to do as he was told—

Well, discipline, the chain of command, had to be main-
tained, didn't it? The management would have to uphold a
clerk against a bellboy. They would have to do it or fire him,
and how could you fire a man for being utterly correct?

So. . .

Fillmore glanced up at the lobby clock. He straightened
his shoulders, and his head reassumed its imperious tilt. . .
Three minutes, no, now it was four minutes. Four minutes
to get a bag out of the checkroom, and he hadn't done it
yet! Now that was fine service for you. That was certainly a
fine way to run a hotel.

He waited until the big hand of the clock jerked again,
marking off another minute. Then, easing open the door of
the desk area, he moved silently down the lobby. Perhaps
he thought, Rhodes was sneaking a smoke, loitering along
the baggage racks while the lady waited. Or perhaps. . .
perhaps he was trying to pull something funny. Trying to

flirt with her. He was a good-looking punk—too darned good-looking to be trustworthy! Probably had the idea that he could crook a finger at a woman, and she'd come a-running.

Fillmore paused at the corner of the areaway, straining his ears to listen. He could hear them—what sounded like an argument—but he couldn't hear what they were saying. The bellboy's voice was strained. The lady's was softly insistent, faintly wheedling.

Fillmore hesitated, teetering in nervous indecision. Perhaps—well, it might be well to go a little slow. Rhodes was something rather special with the hotel management. He had risked his life in the hotel's interests, and if things came to a showdown—

But things wouldn't! He wasn't doing anything out of the way. After all, what was wrong with making an inquiry, intervening, where there was obviously some difficulty between a patron and an employee?

Fillmore patted his tie, threw back his shoulders and stepped around the corner.

"What's going on here?" he said briskly. "What's the trouble, Rhodes?"

Rhodes' face went white. *So he had been up to something!* The woman also seemed perturbed, but she managed a smile. She nodded at the bag, a kind of dispatch case, which the bellboy was holding.

"I've misplaced my baggage check," she said. "Can't I please get the bag without it?"

"Well, I—uh—" Fillmore hesitated.

"Please? My husband just returned to town tonight, and he's very anxious to have these papers. I know it's rather unusual, but I have been a guest here—this bellboy admits he remembers me and. . ."

She looked at Fillmore winningly. He stared uncertainly at Rhodes. He'd had the same problem before at other hotels, and he'd known how to handle it. But at the Manton—well, it might be different here. Rhodes knew what the custom was better than he did.

"Well," he said. "I hardly—you do remember this lady, Rhodes?"

Rhodes hesitated. He said, his voice strangely tight, "I

remember."

"And you can't—I'm not ordering you to, understand—you can't release a piece of baggage without a check? You don't do that under any circumstances?"

"No."

"Not even if the owner identifies the contents?"

"N-no. I mean, she—she—"

"Answer me! Speak up!" Fillmore was sure of himself again. His voice rang with authority. "That is the custom, isn't it?. . . I'm sorry you were delayed, madam, but if you'll just identi—"

"But I already have! I satisfied the boy that it was my bag, but apparently"—she laughed a little wryly—"he wasn't satisfied with the tip I gave him."

"Oh, he wasn't, eh?" Fillmore's lips tightened grimly. "Give me that bag, Rhodes, do you hear me? Give it here instantly?"

Reaching across the counter, he snatched the bag from the bellboy's hand, presented it to the lady with a courteous bow. "I'm extremely sorry about this, madam. May I see you to your cab?"

Murmuring apologies, muttering sternly about the bellboy's conduct, he escorted her out into the lobby. At the steps to the side entrance, she interrupted, laying a hand on his arm.

"He won't lose his job because of this, will he? I'd feel dreadful if I thought he would."

"But, madam. The Manton cannot and will not tolerate discourtesy on the part of—"

"Oh, I'm sure he didn't mean to be discourteous. It was more thoughtlessness than anything else. . . Promise?" She gave his arm a little squeeze. "Promise he won't be fired."

"Well," said Fillmore, and then, grandly, "Very well. I understand that he does need his place here. Has his father, a semi-invalid, depending on him."

"I know," said Marcia Hillis. "I mean, I thought he must be upset about something."

17

Dusty never knew how he got through that night. It seemed endless, and each of the year-long moments was a nightmare of soul-sickening rage, of rage and hate and frustration—repressed, seething inside him, until the mental sickness became physical. He wanted to kill Fillmore, to choke him with his bare hands. He wanted to hide in a dark corner and vomit endlessly. He wanted. . .

He wanted the unattainable. He wanted what he had always wanted—her. And now he was not going to have her. She was Tug's woman, obviously, irrefutably. Everything else had been pretense, all the caresses and the whisperings and the promises. All for Tug, nothing for him. They'd be together now, on their way out of the country together. They'd be laughing—she'd be laughing, as she told how she'd hoodwinked him. He'd been on the point of giving her the satchel. He couldn't bear to see her hurt, to have her think that he didn't trust her. *Goddam, oh, Goddam!* And he'd been just a little suspicious of her last-minute firmness, her insistence, but if she'd kept up the act a moment longer. . .

But it hadn't been necessary for her to keep it up. He hadn't had time to reach a decision. That goddamned stupid Fillmore had butted in, and there'd been nothing to do but let her have the bag. Jesus, what else could he do? Call her bluff? Say that she hadn't identified the contents, and risk Fillmore's taking over, calling the house dick maybe or the manager? He couldn't do that and she knew it, knew that he'd have to do just what he had done. Let her go, and keep his mouth shut. Let her take the money, and herself, to Tug. Tug's money, *his* money— the whole two hundred and thirty-two thousand.

And the terrible part about it was that he couldn't hate her. He tried to, but he couldn't. He wanted her as much—Christ, he wanted her more!—as he ever had.

Still sick and seething, he drove home that morning. A

kind of vicious delight welled up in him as Mr. Rhodes met him at the door, mumbling worriedly about Miss Hillis' absence. He shoved past the old man. He turned and faced him, his pent-up fury spewing out at this easy and defenseless target.

"So she's left. What about it? What business is it of yours, anyway?"

"B-but—" Mr. Rhodes gave him a startled look. "But I—where could she have gone to? Why would she have left, gone away at night, without saying anything? Everything was all right when I went to bed. We'd sat up talking rather late, and then I helped her make down the lounge and—"

"I'll bet you did. It's a goddamned wonder you didn't try to go to bed with her. Christ knows, you haven't left her alone for a second since she's been here!"

"B-but—" The old man's mouth dropped open. "Son, you can't mean—"

"The hell I don't! That's probably why she left, because she couldn't stand the sight of you any more. She had all she could take, just about like I've had all I can take. . .Yes, you heard me right, by God! I'm sick of you, get me? Sick of looking at you, sick of listening to you, sick of—"

The phone rang. Raging, he let it ring on for a moment. And then he snatched up the receiver and almost yelled into the mouthpiece.

A muted chuckle came over the wire. "Something riling you, kid?" said Tug Trowbridge.

Dusty's hand jerked. His fingers went limp, and the receiver started to slide from his grasp.

"Now get this, kid," Tug went on swiftly. "I'll be by the side entrance there tonight, tomorrow morning rather, at one o'clock. Driving, yeah. I'll give three short taps on the horn, and—Dusty! You listening to me?"

"I'm l-lis— You can't!" Dusty stammered. "You—"

"Why not? I'll have this little collapsible bag you can slip under your jacket. You put mine in that, and bring it back out again, just like I'd given you a check on it. What—"

"But I—"

"Yeah?" Tug chuckled again. "Kind of surprised you, huh, thought it would be more complicated? Well, that's it. One o'clock tonight. Three taps on the horn."

"Wait!"

"Yeah? Snap into it, kid."

"I've got to see you," said Dusty. "Something's—I've got to see you!"

"Huh-uh. No, you don't. You just—"

"But I can't! I m-mean—" *He wouldn't dare tell Tug the whole truth. Tug had killed three men for that money, his share of it, and he would not believe the truth if he heard it. He would think that*—"I mean, that's what I've got to see you about."

Heavy silence for a moment. Then, softly, "You wouldn't be hungry, would you, kid? You wouldn't want it all . . . and that ten grand reward besides?"

"No! My God, you know I wouldn't—that I couldn't do that."

"Yeah. Well, just so you know it, too, that you'd hang yourself if you tried it. They nab me and you're sunk, or you try putting the blocks to me and you're—"

"I'm not! It's—I can't explain now, but I've got to see you, *now*—"

"All right," Tug cut in, curtly. "I don't like it, but all right. Same place in about an hour."

The line went dead.

Dusty hung up the receiver, glanced at his father. The old man was slumped down into his chair, staring vacantly into nothingness. There was a stunned look on his face, a look of sickness that transcended sickness in his eyes. He was obviously unaware of the telephone conversation. It had meant nothing to him. Nothing, now, meant anything to him.

Dusty took a bill from his wallet, the first one his fingers touched, and flung it into his lap. A ten-spot, too damned much—anything was too damned much—but he had an idea that it wouldn't be much longer, now; with the props kicked out from under him, the old bastard might have sense enough to die. Meanwhile, it was worth any amount to crack the whip and see him cringe. To toss the bill at him as though it were a bone to a dog.

He waited a moment for the old man to speak—hoping for, wanting the opportunity to shut him up again. Then, as his father remained silent, he slammed out the door and headed for his rendezvous with Tug.

Things could be a lot worse, he thought. Yes, sir, they were not nearly as bad as they had seemed a while ago. He'd lost her, but at least she hadn't gone to Tug. She'd been working for herself, not Tug, and somehow that was not so hard to bear. He'd lost everything he wanted, but the loss had done something for him. It had pushed him to the point of losing, getting rid of, something he didn't want—someone who, he realized now, he had always hated. Yes, hated. Hated, hated, hated! Hated when he had touched her, the woman who was all woman. Hated—hated him—if he even came near her. Hated and wanted him to die. As he probably would die soon, now that he was completely stripped of reason to live.

And perhaps. . . perhaps she was not lost yet: the she reborn in Marcia Hillis. Perhaps, with the ten thousand dollars in reward money, he could find her and. . .

He turned off the highway, crossed over the railway tracks to the abandoned road on the other side. A car was parked just beyond the crest of the first hill. It was old and battered, but there was a look of sturdiness about it and the tires were new. The man behind the wheel was heavily bearded, dressed in faded overalls and jumper, and had an old straw work hat pulled low on his forehead. A sawed-off shotgun lay across his knees. He gestured with it impatiently as Dusty greeted him.

"So you wouldn't have known me. So forget it and start talking. What the hell did you have to see me about?"

Tug cursed. He mopped his face with a blue bandanna handkerchief and went on cursing, pouring profanity through the polka-dot folds until he was strangling and breathless.

"Those bastards! Those stupid, blockheaded sons-of-bitches! Boy, I wish I hadn't already bumped 'em off! I'd like to do it all over again."

"Then you intended to kill her all along," Dusty said. "All that stuff you told me about how much she liked me and how you'd fix things up—"

"You kicking about it?" Tug turned on him fiercely. "You let her screw you for your share of the dough, and you're kicking?"

"I just want to get things straight. If you'd told me the truth in the first place . . ."

"Well, now you got it straight. We'd snatched her, hadn't we? Yeah, I know what you thought, but sure it was a snatch. So naturally she had to be bumped off. And if those stupid jerks had had any sense—" Tug broke off, choking, ripped out another string of curses. I should have known better'n to trust'em with a dame like that. I should have known they'd try to keep her around a while, take her for a few tumbles before they knocked her off."

"But I don't understand. If she got away from them—"

"*If?* What the hell do you mean, if?"

"But why didn't they tell you?"

"Because they didn't know about it, goddammit! She made the break the night of the robbery, while we were all busy at the hotel. It had to 've happened, then. You can see that, can't you, for Christ's sake? If she'd got away before then, there wouldn't have been any hold-up. She'd have yelled to the coppers."

Dusty frowned. He stared out through the grimy windshield at the sun-sparkled pavement. Back in the hillside underbrush a raincrow cawed dryly. A gust of hot wind rolled over the abandoned fields, rattling the yellowed, waist-high weeds.

"She knew all about me," Dusty said. "She knew where the money was, that we hadn't settled on a way of splitting it up. So if she wasn't working with you—"

"Goddammit, does it look like she was? She didn't know nothing—it was just guesswork. She figured we couldn't decide on how to divvy the dough until afterwards. I wouldn't know when you'd be going back to work. I wouldn't know how soon I could get in touch with you and—"

"She couldn't have guessed everything," Dusty said. "She couldn't have guessed that the money would be in the checkroom. Someone told her, that and everything else."

Tug shrugged irritably. "What's the difference? You got screwed, that's the main thing, so that means I take a screwing, too. To hell with her. What the hell difference does it make if—"

"I want to know," Dusty insisted. "I've got to know."

Tug hesitated, shrugged again. "All right. It don't make me look real pretty, but—I guess I don't, anyhow, huh? And it's got no connection with you. I've been playin' pretty rough, but I couldn't cross you if I—"

"Who was she?"

"Bascom's daughter. She was a dancer like I said; that part was on the level. Hillis was her stage name, and—"

"B-Bascom's—his—?"

"You want me to tell you or not? We ain't got all day. Every cop in town is looking for me. Yeah, his daughter. I slapped the truth out of her that morning. He'd had her check in there at the hotel. He'd done everything he could to make you quit and it hadn't worked, so she set you up for the push. She'd accuse you of attempted rape, see, tell you she'd file charges if she ever saw you again. If you got stubborn she'd actually call Bascom—her father, only you wouldn't know that—and the way things would be stacked against you, you'd have to quit. So. . . so that's the way it was, kid. Me and the boys put the snatch on her. Bascom saw that I'd found out about him trying to cross me, and he figured she'd have a lot better chance of living if he got back on the track and stayed there. I kind of let him think that, see? He knew he was a goner himself, whatever happened, and all he could do now was—"

"Bascom," Dusty said slowly. "Why did he want me to quit? Why did he do all that, try so hard to—to—" He broke off, staring at Tug. Tug's eyes shifted uncomfortably. "Oh," he said. Then, "Well. . ."

Tug coughed and spat out the window. He shifted the shotgun slightly, mumbled something about, Christ, the goddamned heat.

"You were going to kill me," Dusty said. "Someone had to be killed and I was supposed to be it."

"What the hell?" Tug said, gruffly. "It was just business, kid, nothing personal. I really wanted it to be Bascom, right from the beginning, but—"

"Yes. He made a better fall guy, didn't he? But why did it have to be him or me? What difference would it have made if I'd quit or got fired and another bellboy had taken my place? You could still have gone right ahead and—"

"Huh-uh. It had to be someone that'd been there quite a while. Someone who knew the ropes and who'd have had time to pal up with me. Nope, if Bascom had got rid of you there wouldn't have been any hold-up. We'd have had to wait until the next racing season, and he knew I couldn't wait."

Dusty nodded. He had no more questions. None, at least, that Tug could answer. She'd spent two days there at the house, talking to him, probing him, watching him. And perhaps she'd been drawn to him, as she'd said; perhaps she'd felt pretty much the same about him as he felt about her. But there'd been some doubts in her mind. She hadn't been sure of his guilt, whether he'd been a willing and knowing accomplice to her father's murder, but neither had she been unsure. So—well, there was the answer: the clue to the exact amount of her sureness and unsureness. She had left him here practically penniless, to face Tug empty-handed with a story which might not be believed. She had been sufficiently sure-unsure to put him on a spot where he might have been killed, or—

Or? Dusty's pulse quickened suddenly. . . Tug. She'd have had no doubts about *his* part in the murder. Tug would have been the guy for her to get, and what better way was there—what other way, rather—than this one? She could only get to Tug through him. By making off with all the dough, she probably figured on—

Nuts. Nothing. It was all a pipedream. She'd wanted the money period. She'd got it period. That was all there was to it. That was as far as she'd thought. Like she'd pointed out, a hundred-odd grand wouldn't last long— only half as long as twice that much. So—

But maybe not! Jesus, maybe the Pipedream was true! And there was nothing to lose by believing in it, nothing to lose regardless. Tug couldn't be told the truth. God, what he might do— would probably do—if he was told! Tug had to die, and—

Tug was watching him, studying him. Dusty lit a cigarette casually and thumbed the match out the window.

"Well?" he said.

"It ain't well," Tug grunted. "It ain't a goddamned bit well, but I guess I got to take it. Christ, if I'd known it was going to turn out this way, all that planning and sticking my neck out for a lousy fifty grand or so—"

"Fifty?" Dusty pretended surprise. "But she only got my half. Yours is still—"

"Who you kiddin'?" Tug glared at him savagely. "You'd just hand it all over and like it, huh? You wouldn't try to pick yourself up a few bucks—about ten thousand of 'em—some other way? Don't crap me, kid. Don't act stupid any more than you have already. You wouldn't play with me any longer'n it paid you, so I'm paying. I'm splitting with you right down the middle."

"Well," Dusty murmured. "I'll, uh, certainly appreciate—"

"Screw your appreciation. Forget it. Just don't pull anything funny, get me? Because maybe I'd get bumped off, but it wouldn't make you anything. They'd want to know why I was there, see, and they'd turn that place upside down to find out. And. . ."

And they wouldn't find anything. They might be suspicious, but they'd have no proof.

"All right," Tug concluded. "You better get going. I'll see you at one tomorrow morning just like I gave it to you over the phone."

"Suppose I can't be there right at one? I might get tied up on a call and—"

"Well, right around one then. Say five minutes of until five minutes after. I'll circle the block until I see you on the floor. And make sure you have my money."

Dusty nodded. He pushed open the door of the car and started to get out. Tug's voice, strangely strained and faltering, brought him to a halt.

"I—I always been nice to you, ain't I, kid? Always treated you like a friend, gave you plenty of dough without never makin' you feel cheap to take it?"

"Yes," Dusty agreed warmly. "You were always swell to me, Tug."

"Maybe it sounds like the old craperoo, now. But, well, I couldn't've gone through with the first deal. The boys thought I was nuts knockin' myself out to take you off the spot and put Bascom on it. It was risky as hell, y'know, and they gave me a pretty bad time about it. But I had to do it. I guess, kid—I know you probably won't believe me —but I guess there probably wouldn't have been any deal if you hadn't agreed to come in. I'd've just taken what dough I had and skipped."

Dusty murmured inaudibly, lowering his eyes to conceal their contempt. So this was the way a hard guy acted, this was the great Tug Trowbridge when the chips were down! Scared stiff, pleading. Whining about friendship.

"I. . . it'll be all right, won't it, kid? You ain't—there ain't no reason why it wouldn't be all right?"

"How"—Dusty hesitated—"how do you mean?"

"I mean I won't be walkin' into a trap. You wouldn't—"

"I couldn't. You know that yourself."

"Yeah, but I been thinkin', kid. If that dame got away with *all* the money. . ." Tug's hands came down on Dusty's shoulders. They gripped fiercely, then gently, humbly. "Just tell me the truth, Dusty. That's all the break I want. She didn't get it *all*, did she?"

Dusty shook his head. He said, "Of course not. Why would I gave it all to her?"

"Don't be afraid to tell me, kid. If that's what happened, just tell me, for God's sake, an'. . ."

"Afraid?" said Dusty, and now it was an effort to hide his disdain. "Why would I be afraid of you. . . Tug?"

Mr. Rhodes was in the kitchen when he reached home. His thin hair was damp from a recent shower, and his face was freshly shaved. He had done the little that he could to make himself presentable, someone not to be ashamed of, and now bustling about the cupboards and stove, he was demonstrating his usefulness, proving that here indeed, aged and ill or not, was an asset.

Dusty stood in the doorway watching him, grinning to himself. Contemptuously amused, his hatred challenged by what he saw. He had left Tug oddly exhilarated, elated and restive; he had been expecting an ordeal with the gangster and his nerves had been keyed for one. And there had been nothing to unkey them, no outlet for the building mass of nervous energy. Tug had been a virtual pushover, almost laughable there at the last. He was as bad as this old fool, still clutching at, fighting for, life— pleading for what he could no longer demand.

"Bill"—the old man kept up his brisk movements, spoke without turning around—"it was all my fault, this morning. You were tired and you've been under a lot of strain, and— well, anything you said, I know you didn't—"

"I meant it," said Dusty. "I meant every goddamned word of it."

"B-But—no! No, you didn't. Why would you—" A cup slid from Mr. Rhodes' hands, clattered and shattered against the sink.

Dusty laughed, jeered. His excitement was fresh water for the old seeds of hatred.

"Would you like to know a little secret, Dad? Would you like to know how your name got on that petition? Well, I'll tell you. I—"

"I—I—" Mr. Rhodes turned around at last. His eyes swept over Dusty, unseeing, blindly, and he moved dully toward the door. "I—I think I'd better lie down," he said. "I—I—"

"Oh, no you don't!" Dusty snapped. "I've been wanting to tell you for a long time, and now, by God, I'm—"

"I already know," the old man said absently. "Your mother—she and I, I think we both must have known right from the beginning, but we couldn't admit it. Now . . . now, I think I'd better lie down. . ."

He entered his bedroom and closed the door.

Later that day, when he had gone to bed, Dusty heard his father wandering around the house, moving back and forth through the rooms, aimlessly at first, then still aimlessly but with a kind of frantic desperation. He heard him leave the house, and, falling asleep, he did not hear him return. But when he left for the hotel that night, the old man was back in his room. Dusty listened at the door for a moment, to the blurred, muffled sounds that seeped through the panels.

It sounded like he was praying. Or singing. Kind of like he was praying and singing together. And occasionally there was something like a sob. . . choked, strangling, rattling.

Dusty went on to the hotel.

At twenty minutes of one, he stepped into one of the lobby telephone booths and made a call to the police.

. . .They took no chances with Tug. They picked him up in their floodlights, from a mezzanine window of the hotel, from a second story window across the street. They shouted to him once. And perhaps he didn't understand the command, perhaps he was too startled to obey it, or perhaps—for he thrust the shotgun through the car window—he was starting to obey it. But the police did not deal in perhapses where Tug Trowbridge was concerned; they were resolving no doubts in his favor.

Five minutes after he drove up to the hotel, he was on his way to the morgue. Within the same five minutes, two detectives were searching the checkroom and two others were escorting Dusty to the police station, and still another two were speeding toward Dusty's house.

They found nothing there, of course; no trace of the loot from the robbery. Only the lifeless body of an old man, and a half-empty bottle of whiskey.

He had met most of the detectives before. They had talked to him at the hospital, visited him so often that they had become friendly, addressing him by his first name or nickname. But there was nothing friendly about them now. Curt and cold, they took turns at the questioning, asking the same questions over and over, making the same accusations over and over. Calling him you and bud and buster or, at best, Rhodes.

He sat on a hard chair under a brilliant light. Their voices lashed out from the shadows, impassive, relentless, untiring.

"Stop stalling. . ."

"We got you cold, bud. . ."

"Tell the truth and we'll make it easy on you. . ."

"Why did Tug want to see you? Come on, come on! you didn't have the loot stashed, why—"

"*I told you!*"

"Tell us again."

"He—all I know is what he said when he called me. Just before I called you. He said he was broke, and he wanted me to help him and—"

"Sure he was broke. He'd left the dough with you, and you wouldn't give him his cut."

"Why'd he come to you for money? What made him think you'd give him any?"

"Come on, come on!"

"I'm trying to tell you! He'd always been pretty nice to me, a lot of big tips, and I suppose he thought—"

"He was a pal of yours, wasn't he? You were like that. Ain't that right? AIN'T THAT RIGHT?"

"No! I mean he was nice to me, but—"

"Yeah. Cut you in on that robbery, didn't he? Made you his inside man, didn't he? Gave you the loot to stash, didn't he? Come on, why don't you admit it?"

"No! I didn't have anything to do with the robbery!"

"Why'd Tug want to see you then?"

"I told you why! I told you all I—"

"Tell us again. . ."

The door of the room burst open, and a man rushed in. "We found it, guys! We found the dough! Right where we thought it would be!"

"Swell. Attaboy!" The detectives congratulated him, turned back to Dusty. "Well, there you are, bud. Stalling won't get you anywhere, now."

"I'm not stalling! I just don't—"

"You heard what the man said. They found the dough there at the hotel."

"They couldn't have! I mean—"

"Yeah, we know. Because you didn't stash it there. Tug thought you did, but you'd sneaked it out."

"I d-didn't!"

"Leave him alone, you guys. Rhodes an' me understand each other. . . Now, look, kid (*whispering*), whyn't you and

me make a little deal, huh? You just give me your word
you'll take care of me, whatever you think's fair, and I'll
make these jerks let you go. We can pick up the loot
together, an'. . . What's the matter? Don't you trust me?"

"I don't know where it is! I didn't have anything to do
with it! I—"

"Aaah, come on. . . Why did Tug want to see you,
then?"

"I told you!"

"Tell us again."

. . .They gave up on him at seven that morning. Around
ten o'clock, he was taken out of his cell and driven to the
courthouse. The two detectives escorting him asked no
questions, seemed almost indifferent to him. While he sat
down on a bench outside the county attorney's office, they
wandered away to the water cooler, stood there chaffing
and joking with a couple of deputy sheriffs.

Dusty looked down at the floor dismally, listening to
them, half listening. He raised his head, startled, then casually moved down to the end of the bench. The door to the
county attorney's office was slightly ajar. He could hear two
men talking inside. Arguing. One of them sounded irritable
and stubborn; the other—the one who apparently was winning the argument— as placatory and resigned.

*"Now, you know I'm right, Jack. We both know that kid is
guilty as hell. He had to be, and the fact that the money has been
returned—"*

*"Every nickel of it, by mail, Bob. And there's no clue to the
sender. Under the circumstances, and regardless of our personal
feelings, we have no case. Our only chance of sticking Rhodes was
in tying him up with the money. Now that its been returned. . ."*

Dusty blinked. The money returned? It must be some
kind of trap. This conversation was for his benefit; they
meant him to hear it, so that—So that?

*"He had an accomplice! When the accomplice saw Rhodes was
in trouble, he—"*

*"But he wasn't in trouble at the time. The package was post-
marked yesterday afternoon."*

*"He mailed it himself, then. That's it! Tug was turning on the
heat, and. . . and, uh. . ."*

"You see, Bob? You're talking in circles. If Rhodes had had the

money, he could have paid off. Tug wouldn't have been turning on the heat, as you put it."

"But—but this just doesn't make sense, Jack. It leaves everything up in the air. Aside from the money, a man was murdered and—"

"You can't separate the one from the other, Bob. And who cares about that clerk, anyway? He was a crook, a fugitive from justice."

"Yes, but goddammit, Jack—"

"I know. There are a lot of loose ends. But they don't lead to Rhodes. They don't, and we can't make them."

"Well. . ."

"The hotel is satisfied. So is the insurance company. As long as they don't want to prosecute, why should we knock ourselves out? We can't win. Ten to one, the thing would never go to trial. He'd get a dismissal before—"

"Yeah. Well (grudgingly), all right. But I'm telling you something, Jack. Maybe we can't stick him on this, but I'm telling you. If that bastard ever pulls anything else—if he even looks like he's going to pull anything else—he's a dead pigeon! I'll hang him, by God, if I have to pull the rope myself!"

"Sure, ha, ha, and I'll help you. I feel the same way."

He no longer had a job. He did not have to be told that he could not return to the Manton. And he did not care particularly—he felt dead, inside, uncaring about everything. But the fact remained that he was now without income, and practically broke. As for that reward on Tug, well, he grimaced at his foolishness in ever expecting to collect that reward. He had started to mention it to that county attorney, just *started* to. And the guy had blown his top. He'd yelled for the other guy to have him thrown back in the can, to throw him in and throw the key away. And the other guy had jerked his head at the door, and told him to beat it while he was still able to.

"You're a lucky boy, Rhodes, but don't lean on it too heavy. The next time we pick you up . . ."

So Dusty had got out of there fast and, now, a dozen blocks away from the courthouse, he was just slowing down. It was almost noon. The humid heat poured over him stickily. His shirt was sweat-stuck to his back, and he felt that he stank with the stench of the jail.

He walked two more blocks to the railroad station, and bathed in one of the men's room showers. He got a shave in the station barber shop, and, afterwards, coffee and toast in the grille. The food stuck in his throat. He was hungry, but it seemed tasteless to him.

Leaving the grille, he moved out into the waiting room, stood uncertainly in its vaulted dimness staring up at a bulletin board. Not that he was going anywhere, of course. How could he? Where would he want to go? He simply stood there, staring blindly, looking not out but inward, puzzled and pitying himself much.

Bascom? Well, Bascom's life was forfeit anyway, wasn't it? Having nothing to lose he could lose nothing. And his father, Mr. Rhodes—well, he too had been a dead man already. Death had simply put an end to futility. And as for Tug Trowbridge, a mass murderer, not worth a second thought, deserving exactly what he had received. And Marcia Hillis. . .

Why? Why, in the name of God, had she done it? What had she hoped to gain by doing it?. . . He had a feeling that long, long ago, he might have understood. But, then, naturally, back there in time, there would have been nothing to understand. The situation would not have been posed then; he would have been incapable of bringing it about. Back there, so long ago, yet such a short time actually, he had been just another college student, and if he had been allowed to go on, if he had been given the little he was entitled to without being impelled to grab for it. . .

He left the railroad station, and walked quickly back toward the business section. He couldn't think about Marcia Hillis—face the riddle and reproach which she represented. He couldn't stop thinking about her.

Why? Why had he been singled out for this black failure, this bottomless disappointment? Why not, for example, some of those loud-mouthed clowns, the office holders and professional patriots, who had advanced themselves by ruining the old man? Mr. Rhodes had said that time, that history, would take care of them. But they had not been taken care of yet; they were still riding high. And he, he who was basically guilty of no more than compromise; he who, instead of fighting circumstance, had tried only to profit from it—

He was no better off than the old man. Alive, yes, but robbed of any reason to live.

. . . He got his car off the parking lot, drove it to a nearby sales lot. It was a good car; the dealer readily admitted its quality. But it seemed that there was just no demand for this particular make and model any more. The public, for mysterious and unreasonable reasons, just didn't want 'em at any price. Of course, if Dusty wanted to get rid of it *bad* enough. . . Dusty did. He accepted five hundred dollars without argument, and caught a bus homeward.

The money would just about take care of the old man's funeral, he supposed. Maybe he could get out of paying for it, but it would be troublesome, no doubt, and he'd had enough trouble for a while. Better get the old bas—better get him buried and forget him. Get it over with the fastest and least troublesome way possible. Probably it would have looked better if he'd gone by the funeral parlor this morning—but to hell with how it looked. He didn't have to care about looks. He was through pretending, and if people wanted to make something out of it, let 'em try.

He got off the bus, started past the little lunchroom-bar which his father had used to patronize. And inside he heard the creaking of stools, sensed the unfriendly eyes staring out at him. It was the same way when he passed the neighborhood grocery store, the barber shop and filling station, the open windows and doors of the dingy houses. Bums, loafers, white trash, scum floating from one day's tide to the next. And they were giving *him* the cold eye!

It couldn't be because he'd been in jail, a prime suspect in a quarter-million-dollar robbery. Jail was no novelty for the habitues of this neighborhood. So it must be because of the old man—they must think that. . . It was unreasonable. They hadn't the slightest grounds for thinking that he had brought about Mr. Rhodes' death. But still, obviously, they did think that. Rather they knew that he had.

He began to walk faster. He was a little breathless when he reached the house, and he almost ran up the steps and into the living room. Relieved, and suddenly ashamed of the feeling, he sank down into a chair. He mopped his face, leaned back wearily with his eyes closed. The room seemed to echo with the beating of his heart, faster and louder, louder and faster, running a deafening race with his breathing, and suddenly frightened, he opened his eyes again. Now he was looking into his father's room—in at the bed. And something was. . . something wasn't, of course, it was only a shadow, but—

He stood up. He backed out of the room, turned toward his own bedroom. And through the half-opened door, stretched out on the bed, he saw another shadow. He closed his eyes, reopened them. It was still there. A shadow, only, only an illusion born of the dimness and his imagination. But he backed away again. He entered the kitchen, and the shades were drawn high there and the sunlight streamed in. But somehow it was worse than the other rooms. He could see too clearly here, and the seeing was worse than the imagining. . . The cupboards, recently rearranged so neatly. The sink, still half filled with dishwater. The shattered cup on the floor. . .

But there was no place else to go. He was will-less to go elsewhere. He stood self-deserted, abandoned to a wilderness of the unbearable. For the wilderness would be everywhere now. It would always be everywhere.

Only she could have taken him out of it, filled the yawning emptiness, imparted meaning, and aroused desire. She could have done that, but only she. Pursuing her, he had climbed deeper and deeper into the pit, only to find nothing at the bottom but. . . but the bottom.

Blindly, he stumbled into a chair. He dropped down at the oilcloth-covered table and buried his face in his arms.

He thought, *"Jesus, I can't stand it!"*

He sobbed out loud, "C-Christ, I can't stand it! I can't stand—"

The floor creaked behind him. He stiffened, choking back a sob, too terrified to look around.

"I know. . ." said Marcia Hillis, "but I'll help you, darling. We'll stand it together."

They were on the lounge. His arms were around her and his face was buried against her breast, and that, to have her again, was all that mattered. He clung to her, wanting nothing more, only half-aware of what she said.

"It's all right," he murmured, over and over. "It doesn't matter."

"You do understand, Dusty? It wouldn't have been any good the other way. To start off like that, with stolen money. . . I know what it does to people. I know what it did to my mother, and my father—"

"It's all right," he said. "I don't care about the money."

"I wanted to ask you to return it. I was so afraid, for you, darling, so terribly afraid of what Tug might do. But I hadn't had time to get to know you, and I had to act quickly. And—and—"

"And you weren't quite sure, were you?" he said. "You felt that I might have killed Bas—that I'd known your dad was going to be killed."

"Well," she nodded reluctantly. "I didn't want to think that, but. . ."

"I don't blame you," he said. "You'd just about have to think that. I was the inside man on the robbery, and how could I be unless I knew that—knew everything that was going to happen? But Tug didn't tell me, Marcia. He didn't have to explain anything to me. He threatened to kill you if I didn't do what I was told. That was all I knew, all I could think about. I was afraid to ask any questions, and—"

"I know, dear." She brushed her lips against his forehead. "It was too late to change plans then, but I knew—I was sure—that last night before I came to the hotel."

"Oh? How do you—"

"Your father. It was the first time we'd been alone together, you know, and all he could talk about was you. The sacrifices you'd made, everything you'd given up for him. How patient you were with him, how kind and generous. So . . . . so I knew, Dusty. I was sure. If you were like that, and I knew that you were, then you couldn't have . . ."

"I—I didn't do much for him," Dusty said. "No more

than I should have."

He was smiling to himself, exulting. Not, of course, because of his deception of her—he was sorry that that was necessary—but because of the broad triumph, the justification, which the deception represented. He had been right, after all. The path into the pit had led not to emptiness but fullness.

". . . heart failure, Dusty? The story in the morning paper was pretty vague."

"Heart failure induced by alcohol. That's what the police said. You see, the doctor didn't want him to know how sick he was, and as long as he'd never gone to any excesses, why. . .." He explained, his voice muffled against the material of her dress. "It was my fault partly, I guess I knew he was feeling very depressed, and if I'd just bought him what he needed instead of giving him the money—"

"Don't! You mustn't feel that way, darling."

"Well. . . If I'd had any idea at all that—"

"Of course. You don't need to tell me that." She kissed him again, murmured on soothingly, reassuringly. . . When you loved someone you were sometimes too good for them for their own good. She knew how that was, how it had been with her father. "He thought a great deal of you, too, Dusty. He thought you were, well, not weak exactly, but a little too easy-going. But—"

Dusty nodded, humbly. He thought, *I'll have to get her out of this neighborhood fast. Get her away before any of these bastards talked to her.*

His arms tightened around her fiercely. Even the thought of losing her was terrifying. God, she couldn't find out the truth. He'd rather die than have her find out. He would die.

He held her, tighter and tighter, and still he could not get close enough to escape the fear. There was only one escape from that—there had never been but one escape from The Fear—and. . . And she laughed, tenderly, and leaned back. She lay back on the lounge, pulling him with her.

"Yes, Dusty! Yes, darling!" she said, and her voice was eager. And, then, right at that long-waited-for moment, she suddenly frowned and pushed him away. "Dusty! Someone's stopped out in front."

"What? To hell with 'em" he said. "Just—"

"Don't! We can't!" She sat up firmly. "Who is it, Dusty?"
He released her reluctantly. He turned and looked
through the curtains, cursed under his breath. It was a
small black sedan. He didn't recognize the man behind the
wheel, although he had a vaguely familiar look about him.
But the man getting out of the car was Kossmeyer.

"My dad's lawyer," he grunted. "Now what the hell does
he want?"

"Well. . ." She looked at him, a trace of a frown on her
face. "He might want any number of things. After all, with
your father dead. . ."

"Yeah. But, right now. Why the hell does he have to come
now?"

The frown disappeared. Her eyes softened again with
tenderness. And promise. And she kissed him swiftly. "I
know, but it'll be all the better, darling. You'll see. I'll be
waiting for you, waiting and ready, Dusty, and. . ."

She was gone, back into his bedroom. Frowning, he
arose and went to the front door.

"Well," he said, curtly. "What do you want?"

"Maybe," said Kossmeyer, "I want to give you ten thousand dollars. Or maybe twenty thousand. Or maybe. . ."

He opened the screen and came in. He sat down and
crossed his short legs, cocked an eyebrow expectantly at
Dusty. Hesitantly, his pulse quickening, Dusty also sat
down.

She hadn't closed the bedroom door. If Kossmeyer got
nasty, she'd—But he could fix that, explain it. Kossmeyer
had tried to take advantage of the old man. He'd put a
stop to it, and the attorney had gotten sore at him.

"What do you mean?" he said. "Why should you want to
give me ten or twenty thousand dollars?"

"We-el," Kossmeyer shrugged, "of course, I'm using the
verb advisedly. I represent your dad's insurers, Rhodes.
They're a client of mine."

"His insurers?" Dusty stared at him blankly. "What—?"

"Yeah, you know, the one he carried a policy with. Ten
thousand dollars, double indemnity. We got kind of a little
problem on it"—Kossmeyer raised his voice as Dusty
started to interrupt. "Kind of a little problem. He died of

heart failure, y'see, a natural cause. But the condition was brought on by, well, let's call it poison; that's what it actually was so far as he was concerned. In other words, the death could be construed as being an unnatural one, in which case, of course, the double indemnity clause would become applicable. Now—"

"Wait! Wait a minute!" Dusty raised his own voice. "You've made a mistake. Dad didn't have any insurance."

"He didn't, huh? You didn't know about it, huh?"

"Of course, he didn't!"

"Well," said Kossmeyer. "Well, let's see now." And he took a folded sheaf of papers from his pocket and smoothed them out against his knee. "According to our records, the records of the Great Southern and Midwest States Insurance Company, your father took out this policy approximately four years ago. You were entering college about that time, and I gather that he wanted to make sure of your education. Also, of course, he—"

Dusty laughed hoarsely, angrily. He said, "I'm telling you you're wrong. I remember when he took that policy out. My mother was the beneficiary, not me. Anyway—"

"Your mother was the beneficiary," Kossmeyer nodded equably. "Naturally, she'd give you such help as you needed, and she was able to give. And, naturally, in the event that her death preceded your father's, the insurance would simply become part of his estate. It wasn't necessary to name you the alternate beneficiary. When he died you'd inherit that estate. . . as, of course,"—the attorney looked up—"you were fully aware."

He waited. After a long moment, he said, "You don't seem very happy, Rhodes. You're the sole heir to a nice juicy wad, and you don't seem at all happy about it. It's kind of surprising, y'know. Certain recent events considered, I'd have said you were pretty hungry for dough."

"W-what—what do you mean by that?"

"Mean? Well, just that there's some other people around town that aren't very happy either. The hotel and their bonding company, and the county attorney. They kind of feel that they had their noses rubbed in it, know what I mean? They had to take it, but it left 'em pretty unhappy. . . But getting back to this insurance policy—"

"He didn't have one! It had lapsed! For God's sake, wouldn't I know if—if—" Dusty caught himself.

Kossmeyer grinned, and nodded again. "That's right, Rhodes. You'd know, all right. Your dad was pretty well along in years when he took that policy out, and he wasn't in the best of health. He had to pay a premium of almost one hundred and fifty dollars a month. And when he didn't have it to pay, when he had to depend on you. . ."

"I didn't pay it! I—"

"No. You gave him the money, and let him pay it. It had to be that way. The only money he had was what you gave him."

"But I tell you—Oh," Dusty said. "So. . . so that's what he did with it. I thought he was giving the money to you."

"Me? Why would I have dunned him, when I knew he didn't have it? The only payment I ever received was that one small retainer you gave me back at the start of the case."

"But that day I talked to you, you said—"

"I said that our expenses had been high. I didn't need to tell you that they hadn't been paid. . . What are you trying to hand me, Rhodes?" Kossmeyer grimaced cynically. "You knew where that money was going. Suppose he could have—from what I hear, I know damnned well you wouldn't have let him—but suppose he could have coaxed the dough out of you a few bucks at a time. Why would he want to anyway? What would be his purpose? The insurance was for your benefit. Why wouldn't he have told you about it?"

"I—I don't—"

But he did know, of course. The old man had been afraid to tell him. He hadn't wanted to admit his fear; probably, he had never admitted it consciously. But still the fear and distrust had been there: the knowledge that someone he loved—someone he had to love and be loved by—might be tempted to kill him.

And now?

Dusty brought a thoughtful frown to his face. Over his inner turmoil, he spread a shell of composure. Kossmeyer couldn't prove anything. He had said nothing yet that could not be explained on the grounds of personal malice.

The thing now was to stop arguing with him, close the door on his insinuations. Otherwise. . .

He closed his mind on the alternative. She had heard nothing thus far that was even mildly damning. She would hear still less than that from now on.

"I wonder," he said, thoughtfully. "I wonder why Dad did that. I suppose. . . well, he probably thought I wouldn't let him make the sacrifices he had to if I'd known about it. He—"

"Sacrifices? With your dough?"

"It was as much his as mine. Anything I had was his, and—"

"It was, huh?" Kossmeyer's eyes glinted savagely. "Horseshit! I've talked to your neighbors around here! I've talked to the people you trade with. I've talked to your doctor. And I've got the same damned story out of every mother's son! That poor devil didn't have two dimes to rattle together. You never did a thing for him that you could get out of doing. It was a disgrace, by God, and the pitiful part about it was the way he stuck up for you— told everyone what a swell guy you were when a blind man could see that—"

"That's a lie! I don't care what anyone says, I—" Dusty paused, forced down the rising tide of panic. "I know what people probably say," he went on, "but it just isn't true. I gave him plenty of money, and I didn't pin him down as to how he spent it. I didn't know he was using it for those insurance premiums. I—why, my God, don't you see how the two things fit together? The one explains the other. The fact that he—that he went around like he did proves that he was using the money I gave him to pay for the insurance."

"Yeah? It don't prove anything like that to me!"

"But don't you see? If he'd used the money for himself, like I meant him to, he—he—"

He paused helplessly. He couldn't express the thought, present it as the pure truth that it was. But Kossmeyer must see it. Kossmeyer was an expert at separating truth from lies, and he must know that—that— Dusty gasped, his eyes widening in sudden and terrified understanding. He had chosen to play the game on the strict grounds of proof: to disregard the rules of right and wrong, truth and falsehood. Now Kossmeyer was playing the same way. Kossmeyer knew that he was guilty, of the old man's death and more. He *knew*, and as long as there were no rules to the game. . .

Kossmeyer. Just one little man, one small voice that could not be cried down. That was all, but in the world of bend-and-be-silent his littleness became large; he stood a Colossus, the little man, and the small voice was as thunder. Kossmeyer. He was retribution. He was justice, losing every game but the last one.

He said:

"At approximately nine o'clock last night, Rhodes, your father bought a fifth gallon of whiskey. You encouraged him to buy it, knowing full well that it would kill him. . ."

"No! I—"

"Where did he get the money then? He'd never had any such sum before. Never more than just enough for the barest necessities of life!"

"He did! He had plenty! I told you—"

". . . just barely enough. He returned to the house around nine-twenty—Yeah, I can prove all this. I been checking on you since I got the news flash early this morning and I can prove every goddamned bit of it!"

"But they're lying! They don't like me around here! They think that I—"

"You're telling me what they think?" Kossmeyer leaned forward grimly. "Save it. I heard enough already to make me sick. . . You left the house at approximately ten-fifteen. Aside from what anyone might say, you had to leave at about that time to get to the hotel and into your uniform by eleven. Between eleven and eleven-thirty, according to a sworn statement of the medical examiner, your father died. In other words, he was in very bad shape, near the point of death, when you left the house. Now"—the attorney suddenly smacked a fist in his palm— "now, Rhodes. Perhaps you can tell me this. You say you didn't want your father to die, and yet he was dying before you left for work. He might easily have been saved by prompt medical attention. So I ask you, Rhodes"—*smack*— "I demand to know, Rhodes"—*smack, smack*— "why you did not intervene to save his life? Why,instead, you walked callously out of the house and left this helpless old man to die!"

Dusty licked his lips. He stared at Kossmeyer, staring beyond this moment and into the one that must certainly succeed it. . . *The courtroom. The coldly knowing eyes. The thundered question, Why, Rhodes? Why didn't you, Rhodes? And the smacking fist, the hammering fist, building a gallows.*

She was hearing all this. Unless he could say something, think of something, she would have to believe it. . .

"I—I didn't know," he said. "I didn't see him before I left."

"Oh." Kossmeyer appeared crestfallen. "Well! He was in his room, huh? He had his door closed and you didn't want to disturb him?"

"Y-Yes! Yes, that's right."

"Uh-hah. I see. But if the door was closed, how did you know he was in the room?"

"Well, I—I could kind of hear him, you know."

"Yes? How do you mean you could hear him?"

"I—I mean, I—"

Kossmeyer was grinning again. Suddenly, briefly, Dusty's terror became cold fury.

"To hell with you! I haven't done anything! I don't have to answer your questions!"

"Sure, you don't," Kossmeyer said. "We can let the county attorney ask 'em. That's one of his boys I got out in the car."

"Well, I. . ." The county attorney. Kossmeyer and the county attorney. They'd had to take lies for truth, and now they would make truth into lies. He'd set the rules for the game, and now. . . "I spoke to him," he said. "I called goodnight to him!"

"Oh?" Kossmeyer was puzzled, he was astonished. "Then you weren't afraid of disturbing him? You knew he was awake?"

"Yes! I mean, well, I wasn't sure. I just called to him softly, and—and—"

"And he answered you? He said good night, son, or something of the kind? I'd say he must have. Otherwise, since you say you could hear him, he was audible to you through a closed door—otherwise, you'd have been alarmed. You'd have looked in on him."

"Well. . .?"

Dusty started to shake his head. He changed the shake to a nod. "Y-Yes. He answered me."

"What did he say?"

"W-What. . . ? Well, just goodnight. Goodnight, Bill."

"Now, I wonder," said Kossmeyer. "Now, I wonder if you couldn't be mistaken. The man was right at death's doorstep. He was in the throws of alcoholic coma. And yet, when you addressed him, he replied to you. He responded in such a way that—"

"All right, then! I guess—maybe I didn't tell him good night! I didn't speak to him! I just heard him in there, I knew he was all right and—"

"But he wasn't all right!"

"Well I—I mean, it sounded like he was. I could hear him snoring—"

"You *could?*" Kossmeyer's astonishment was grotesque. "I know any number of doctors who will be very surprised at that statement. They'll tell you that anything resembling somnolence would have been impossible at the time in question. His physical suffering would have been too great, his mental state too chaotic. . ."

Was it true or not? Must it have been that way, and no other? He didn't know. Only Kossmeyer knew, and the game had no rules.

"I'll tell you what you heard, Rhodes. I'll show you. . ."

"N-No! Don't!"

"Yes," said Kossmeyer. "He'd been poisoned. He was in agony, out of his mind, and—"

His face sagged. Its lines became aged and gentle, and then they tightened, and the folds of skin swelled outward. He swallowed. His neck veins stood out like ropes. A thin stream of spittle streaked down from the twisted mouth, and he gasped and there was a rattle in his throat—a sound overlaid by other sounds. Mumbled, muttered, crazily jumbled yet hideously meaningful. And the gasping rattle, the rattle and the choking. The choking. . .

Dusty closed his eyes. The sounds stopped, and he opened them again. Kossmeyer was standing. He jerked his head toward the door.

"You made one mistake, Rhodes! One big mistake. You

didn't figure on having to tangle with me."

"But I didn't! I m-mean, you know I didn't kill him! I didn't know about the whiskey or the insurance policy—"

"You'll have a chance to prove it. Come on!"

"Come—? W-Where?"

Not that it mattered now. For he had heard it at last, the terrible sound he had been waiting to hear. The closing of a door. Softly but firmly. Finally.

Shutting him out of her life forever.

"Where?" said Kossmeyer. "Did you say where, Rhodes?"

Kossmeyer's legs were very close together; they seemed fastened together. And his hands were behind him, as though pinioned. His head sagged against his chest, drooped on a neck that was suddenly, apparently, an elongated rail of flesh. And gently, as a light breeze rustled the curtains, his body swayed.

He was hanging.

He was hanging.

In the quiet, summer-bright room, Dusty saw himself hanged.

About the Author

James Meyers Thompson was born in Anadarko, Oklahoma, in 1906. He began writing fiction at a very young age, selling his first story to *True Detective* when he was only fourteen. In all, Jim Thompson wrote twenty-nine novels and two screenplays (for the Stanley Kubrick films *The Killing* and *Paths of Glory*). Films based on his novels include: *Coup de Torchon (Pop. 1280)*, *Serie Noire (A Hell of a Woman)*, *The Getaway*, *The Killer Inside Me*, *The Grifters*, and *After Dark, My Sweet*. A biography of Jim Thompson will be published by Knopf.

THE KILLER INSIDE ME

In a small town in Texas, there is a sheriff's deputy named Lou Ford, a man so dull that he lives in clichés, so good-natured that he doesn't even lay a finger on the drunks who come into his custody. But then, hurting drunks would be too easy. Lou's sickness requires other victims—and will be satisfied with nothing less than murder.

0-679-73397-3/$9.00

NOTHING MORE THAN MURDER

Sometimes a man and a woman love and hate each other in such equal measure that they can neither stay together nor break apart. Some marriages can only end with murder. And some murders only make the ties of love and hatred stronger.

0-679-73309-4/$9.00

POP. 1280

As high sheriff of Potts County, a godless, loveless hellhole in the American South, Nick Corey spends most of his time eating, sleeping, and avoiding trouble. If only people would stop pushing Nick around. Because when Nick is pushed, he begins to kill. Or to make others do his killing for him. The basis for the acclaimed French film noir, *Coup de Torchon*.

0-679-73249-7/$8.95

SAVAGE NIGHT

Is Carl Bigelow a fresh-faced college kid or a poised hit man tracking down his victim? And if Carl is really two people, what about everyone around him?

0-679-73310-8/$8.00

A SWELL-LOOKING BABE

The Manton looks like a respectable hotel. Dusty Rhodes looks like a selfless young man working as bellhop. The woman in 1004 looks like a slumming angel. But sometimes looks can kill—as Jim Thompson demonstrates in this vision of crime novel as gothic.

0-679-73311-6/$8.00

Available at your local bookstore, or call toll-free to order:
1-800-733-3000 (credit cards only). Prices subject to change.

VINTAGE CRIME

VINTAGE CRIME / **BLACK LIZARD**

___ **The Far Cry** by Fredric Brown $8.00   0-679-73469-4

___ **His Name Was Death** $8.00   0-679-73468-6
     by Fredric Brown

___ **I Wake Up Screaming** $8.00   0-679-73677-8
     by Steve Fisher

___ **Black Friday** by David Goodis $7.95   0-679-73255-1

___ **The Burglar** by David Goodis $8.00   0-679-73472-4

___ **Cassidy's Girl** $8.00   0-679-73851-7
     by David Goodis

___ **Night Squad** by David Goodis $8.00   0-679-73698-0

___ **Nightfall** by David Goodis $8.00   0-679-73474-0

___ **Shoot the Piano Player** $7.95   0-679-73254-3
     by David Goodis

___ **Street of No Return** $8.00   0-679-73473-2
     by David Goodis

___ **Shattered** by Richard Neely $9.00   0-679-73498-8

___ **After Dark, My Sweet** $7.95   0-679-73247-0
     by Jim Thompson

___ **Cropper's Cabin** $8.00   0-679-73315-9
     by Jim Thompson

___ **The Getaway** $8.95   0-679-73250-0
     by Jim Thompson

___ **The Grifters** $8.95   0-679-73248-9
     by Jim Thompson

___ **A Hell of a Woman** $8.95   0-679-73251-9
     by Jim Thompson

VINTAGE CRIME / **BLACK LIZARD**

___ **The Killer Inside Me** $9.00   0-679-73397-3
     by Jim Thompson

___ **Nothing More Than Murder** $9.00   0-679-73309-4
     by Jim Thompson

___ **Pop. 1280** by Jim Thompson $8.95   0-679-73249-7

___ **Recoil** by Jim Thompson $8.00   0-679-73308-6

___ **Savage Night** $8.00   0-679-73310-8
     by Jim Thompson

___ **A Swell-Looking Babe** $8.00   0-679-73311-6
     by Jim Thompson

___ **The Burnt Orange Heresy** $7.95   0-679-73252-7
     by Charles Willeford

___ **Cockfighter** $9.00   0-679-73471-6
     by Charles Willeford

___ **Pick-Up** by Charles Willeford $7.95   0-679-73253-5

___ **The Hot Spot** $8.95   0-679-73329-9
     by Charles Williams

Available at your bookstore or call toll-free to order: 1-800-733-3000.
Credit cards only. Prices subject to change.